KILL THE WILD

KILL THE WILD

THE HEINOUS CRIMES OF SARA SLICK™ BOOK 2

ST BRANTON   CM RAYMOND   LE BARBANT

DISRUPTIVE IMAGINATION

LMBPN Publishing
PMB 196, 2540 South Maryland Pkwy
Las Vegas, NV 89109

First US edition, June, 2020
Version 1.01, June 2020
ebook ISBN: 978-1-64202-988-8
Print ISBN: 978-1-64202-989-5

THE KILL THE WILD TEAM

Thanks to our Beta Readers
Larry Omans, Kelly O'Donnell, Rachel Beckford

Thanks to our JIT Readers

Daniel Weigert
Paul Westman
Deb Mader
Angel LaVey

Editor

"We can't lose momentum." Hobbes sighed. "This is a critical time, and we need to keep pushing."

Aldrich flicked an unsure look across the room toward Hobbes. The only light in the stone room came from the flames flickering in the fireplace. They cast long shadows across the floor that stretched and undulated with the sweep of long robes as Hobbes stalked back and forth in front of him.

Documents and pages of communication spread out across the table chronicled their plans so far, but the sharp point of his quill hovered above a new, blank sheet. Poised to record whatever Hobbes might say, the Philosopher watched a drop of ink slip from the end and splash onto the cream-colored page.

"It's been difficult, Hobbes. We haven't been able to follow through with our operations the way we intended. The Guild is on high alert now with Sara Slick out of The Deep."

Hobbes stopped pacing and crossed to the table to stare

into the Philosopher's eyes. "I can handle them. How is the rest of the plan progressing?"

The Philosopher drew a breath as he scanned the papers around him. "We're nearly ready."

Hobbes grinned and went back to pacing. This time, excitement and anticipation fueled his short steps rather than anger and frustration. Aldrich stayed in place at the table, ready to take notes or send communications. He knew Hobbes was right.

They couldn't lose momentum. Despite the slowed progression under the watchful, scrutinizing eyes of the Philosophers, the plan was coming together, and it was almost time.

"I'm particularly proud of this plan," Hobbes replied. "The humans are setting the trap for themselves."

CHAPTER ONE

This is so unfair.

It repeated in my head like a bitter mantra. So. Un. Fair.

I dug my heels into the concrete and narrowly avoided running into a glassblower who was not only in the middle of the sidewalk but was currently making a giant wine glass. Beside him was a table where several various-sized glasses already stood, but this one, at least three feet tall, was the largest of them.

A reveler from inside the bar next to him came out, grabbed a glass from the table, threw some bills in his general direction, and wandered toward the next bar.

Delightful chaos, that's what this party was, and I was stuck chasing down Farsiders instead of drinking and eating and dancing with the guy in a giraffe suit. Or was it a dinosaur suit? I couldn't tell, mostly because the costume was coming apart at the seams, and the person inside was more concerned with lifting the head to get more booze in him.

Man, it looked like fun.

But no, not for me. I had to find two or possibly three Farsiders bent on causing trouble at a street carnival where everyone else focused on partying. At least Splinter seemed to be enjoying himself. He wiggled his way up to hang out of my pocket as I ducked under a rope that was the only barrier between the *incredibly professional* Ferris wheel operator and the raucous crowd, then snatched a piece of popcorn from someone's bag and ducked back into my pocket with his treasure.

I waited for the ride operator to say something, but he didn't notice as I passed him and dipped between the ride and a funnel cake stand. For a brief second, the allure of blowing off my responsibilities and sitting in the middle of the street while covering my face in fried dough made me pause, but I pushed on.

"I promise we will get a funnel cake later," I said to Splinter, but really, mostly to myself.

Flickering lights guided me to the other side of the street, where a carnival barker stood outside a giant tent. A sign beside him advertised wonders sure to fill me with amazement, but considering my entire life was seeing wonders that amazed me in the worst way possible, I had less interest in him than in the hot dog stand next to him. Or the fizzy drink of the person who passed me, with the jaunty little hat on the straw. Everything about this festival was the kind of thing I'd rather be doing.

Ever since my time in The Deep, I had longed for days like this, where instead of three dank walls and bars that kept me locked up, I could be the carefree teenager I was before they brought me there. But not yet, not until I had cleared my name at least. Until then, Sara Slick was stuck watching other people have all the fun.

Then I saw a flash of darkness. No, deeper than that. More. Like the darkness other darkness feared. The kind that hides in the closet and scares the most intimidating of monsters. It was quick but unmistakable. The type of darkness that only emanates off the evilest of creatures. Something low and dirty and brutal. Something from The Far.

"Found you, asshole," I muttered. Hot dogs would have to wait.

My feet pounded on the pavement as I tore off after the streak of midnight that had ducked back into the crowd. I silently thanked myself for investing in some decent running shoes before this adventure as I bounded up the side of a lean-to stand to get a better look. Scanning the crowd was easier from up higher, and I occasionally glimpsed the dark figure as it ducked inside large groups of people, then popped up somewhere else. It was like Whack-A-Mole of the damned.

Wherever it vanished from, there was rustling. People cried out like someone had kicked their shin or grabbed their wallet or tripped them unexpectedly. Whatever it was, it was a troublemaker, and I had to catch it before it started something I couldn't stop. I hopped down off the stand and landed at the entrance of a funhouse.

I groaned at the lost opportunity to stare in mirrors that made me look taller as I ran for the edge of the crowd, hoping to circle around and cut the creature off at the pass. It disappeared before I got halfway down the line, and I cursed myself for losing it. I rounded a corner, trying to avoid a wall of teenagers, when a hand grabbed me by the arm.

I yelled in surprise and my fist stopped mere inches from Ally's unflinching and perhaps unaware face.

"Sara, it's over here," she yelled over the sound of the eight-piece band that had begun blasting a swing song somewhere close by.

"Damn, Ally, I almost knocked you out." My hand unclenched as I looked in the direction she was pointing.

"Oh, you wouldn't hit me," Ally said in the tone of a person sure that such a thing would be impossible.

"I wouldn't be so sure—" The rest of my sentence condensed into a surprised yelp as she yanked me in the direction she'd pointed.

"It went down this way," she yelled with a giggle in her voice. She loved this. She might not be much of a fighter, but she loved the chase and the intrigue. Her hastily pulled-back ponytail bobbed in front of me as I jogged after her. My best friend was a great investigative journalist and had led me to this lead about troublemakers from The Far, but she was still as much the kid she was when the Philosophers sent me to The Deep. Her sense of glee from adventure was infectious.

We rounded a corner, and I saw three huddled figures in the distance, all wearing gray hooded sweatshirts and acting like they had something to hide. Something about it wasn't right, but I didn't have too much time to think. They had spotted me.

"Gig's up, douchebags," Ally yelled after them before I could open my mouth. It was like she'd read a book on how to be a 90s action star. I shook my head.

"What she said," I shouted as I snapped out my switch-blade and activated it.

"Aw, fuck," one of them yelled and took off. As he did, his hood fell, and so did his baseball cap. The other two stood petrified on the spot, and I saw their faces. They looked like teenagers. And the smell coming off of them most certainly smelled like pot.

One of them reached into his pocket and I was on him instantly, yanking his arm out and looking for a weapon. It was a lighter. The kid's eyes never left mine, and his mouth formed an 'o' shape as he shook his head and backed away. I let go of his arm and he dropped the lighter at my feet.

"Just say no," Ally shot from behind me, and I hung my head while listening to the footsteps of the kids running away.

"Did you watch a *Law and Order* marathon or something?"

"Come on, Sara, what good is being a hero if you don't get to try out a few one-liners?" She laughed, obviously having the time of her life.

I bent and grabbed the lighter, examining it just in case. I flicked the flint and a small, pitiful flame shot up. I let it go and tossed it at Ally.

"It's here. I know it." I pulled a rune from my pocket. Ally always had good intel, and if she said there was Farside activity here, then there damn well was. And where there was Farsider activity, there might be a clue that could lead back to Hobbes.

"New gift from Archie?" Ally looked entranced by the tool, as if it was a new toy I had gotten for Christmas.

"New and untested." I showed her the flat face set in a

dark blue crystal. The face was copper metal and had the four directions carved in the appropriate places. "Acts like a compass to track Farsiders. The needle is a bone I took off a troll. Nasty bastard, he was."

"Well, I mean, you took his finger. I would expect him to be a little less than pleasant," Ally pointed out.

"He wasn't nice before that." I watched it spin. "Come on, come on," I pleaded, trying to encourage it. It might have worked. I'd seen enough runes to believe some of them had minds of their own. It spun several times but kept landing on north, then spinning.

"Hey, it looks like that troll is giving you the finger." Ally broke into fresh laughter. "A little late, but still effective."

I was about to throw the damn thing at her when it suddenly stopped and showed southwest.

"Got it." I took off running.

Ally lagged, but it was on purpose. I didn't want her rushing into the fight while making bad jokes and warning the Farsider that I was coming. I scanned the crowd in the direction the rune pointed, focusing on dark shapes. Then I saw them. Not one. Three. They seemed to fade into and out of the darkness like they were ebbing and flowing with the tide. One of them elbowed the other, and their heads all turned toward me before they slid into the crowd.

I hoped they didn't think they were blending in well. There were costumes at the festival that showed some serious lack of judgment and sewing know-how, but these took the cake. The horribly disguised figures made themselves look *more* suspicious in the strange layers of multicolored fabric draped haphazardly around their bodies.

They looked like unicorns somebody tossed in a blender with a little pinch of bat-shit crazy.

Exactly the kind of thing I liked to see when hunting down Farsiders frolicking among the innocent humans.

I ducked behind a taco stand. It provided enough cover to throw off the three beings so I could follow them more easily. It also made my stomach rumble in protest as the glorious smell of tacos drifted up my nostrils and into my soul. My head tipped around the side briefly to look around for Ally, catching her as she reached me. We scanned the crowd for the cotton candy disasters. I glimpsed one of them break into a run.

CHAPTER TWO

Whatever these creatures were, they were impossibly fast. The reports coming in were a little hard to believe, but without evidence to the contrary, I had to go with it. Merpeople. Specifically, flesh-eating merpeople, which I didn't know was a thing, but somehow didn't surprise me. Nearly everything from The Far seemed to be flesh-eating these days, and underwater creatures always seemed untrustworthy, anyway. Something about the scales.

All those news reports about people floating around in the ocean and coming back with flesh-eating bacteria? Not bacteria. They got nibbled on by those merpeople.

The three were sticking together, so that was a plus. Although they were weaving through the crowd of people, diving behind stands, then appearing further down the main street or sliding between the legs of a dude on stilts, they hadn't split up yet. Considering it was only Ally and me, and Ally wasn't exactly prepared for a fistfight with a fish, the only way to wrangle them all was to get them together. My switchblade was cold in my pocket, reminding me it was there and ready for action.

Ally lagged a little, and I turned back.

"Find somewhere high up and look for me," I shouted, then kept up my pursuit. I chanced a glance back a few feet away and saw her bent over with one hand on her knee and her head hanging low while panting. Her other hand gave me a thumbs-up. Splinter had jumped ship too, and had his head inside her jacket pocket, his tiny feet kicking to get himself inside. There was also a mysterious candy apple-sized bulge in that pocket.

Good. No distractions.

A group of people staggering into one another after having their fair share and more of the craft beer tent nearby provided a challenge. Rather than run through them or try to get around them, I made a small spectacle of myself and ran up the wall. I launched myself into a half-crouch and hit the wall with my legs still churning. It was a trick that Solon taught me long before, usually as a fancy distraction or a way to get behind an attacker. This time, I used it to vault over some drunken partygoers and to clear the sign hanging above them that read 'CHARLESTON NIGHT OF LIGHTS.'

After landing on my feet, it disappointed me that no one seemed to notice. I'd hoped it would amaze them that a superhero jumped over their heads, but instead, they were still off in their little world of alcohol and poor decisions. What good was doing super cool stuff if no one ever saw it?

"Slick, over there," I heard shouted above me, and I looked up to see Ally. She'd commandeered a pair of stilts and was pointing at a large red tent. She quickly lost her grip and ended up tossing one stilt to the side, then rode the other with both hands until she landed hard on the concrete. In the ever-present state of mind that a street carnival creates, partygoers cheered her on as she fell. As quickly as they became enamored by her, they lost interest and went back to whatever they'd been doing before the entertainment.

"That sucked." She stood and brushed herself off. A wad of gum had stuck to her shirt, and she carefully peeled it off.

"Stilts?"

"I can see everything," she informed me.

"Yeah, but where the hell did you find them?"

"He wasn't using them." She matter-of-factly pointed back at a young man wearing the stilt walkers' costume, but far busier chatting up the girl at one of the booths.

"Fair." I broke into a run for the tent.

When we arrived at the canvas flap, I saw shapes illuminated by light from within. They looked like the shapes I'd seen in the crowd. Tall, somewhat menacing, and vaguely effeminate.

I turned to Ally, drew a deep breath, and pulled the switchblade from my back pocket. "Okay, we got 'em. Follow my lead."

I flipped the canvas door open, fully expecting to hear a loud and dubiously funny quip from Ally, but none came. Instead, there was a hushed silence. Three tall, hooded figures stood in the center of the room like they'd been waiting for us. Wooden crates filled the tent, some with their tops open and cylindrical objects poking out of them.

Before I could hazard a guess about what the hell was in the crates, the figures removed their hoods. Cheap plastic masks with elastic bands strapping them to their faces greeted us in the visage of a colorful mermaid. We had gone from unicorn explosion to plastic mermaids. Fantastic.

Then it occurred to me. This was what Ally's investigations and the millions of hours of conspiracy video on streaming sites had meant by flesh-eating merpeople? They looked between each other and reached under the masks, then pulled them up and off in unison. A deep gasp from behind me filled the silence as we came into eye contact with the revealed creatures.

"Fae…" Ally whispered, transfixed.

"Fae," I confirmed, lead in my voice. But not the fun children's book kind. They could be vicious, even if they weren't technically evil. Chaotic neutral almost, with a dash of the old evil tossed in. "Wait. How did you know they were Fae?"

"Briefly held theory about your disappearance," Ally told me.

"Silly Sara Slick got lost in a tent, and now she's found some Fae," the apparent leader of the group sang at me like a nursery rhyme. Her doe eyes and soft, child-like features hid that she was capable of mass destruction at the drop of a hat. Their wings fluttered behind them in excitement, and it enchanted Ally. They were her type, so it shouldn't have surprised me. Tall, thin, and looking not unlike David Bowie with a long white wig, they were almost androgynous, and their movements were effeminate but sure, even in boredom. They exuded a sense of coolness that I was jealous of, even when they opened their mouths and spoke like a first-grader who was told they couldn't hog all the crayons. "But who's this beside her, is she a Nearsider? Either way, she'll taste the same."

"I'll take the spider and curds and whey, thanks," I spat at her.

All three of them suddenly bared their sharp, pointed teeth, then giggled and ran off. The teeth were enough to snap Ally out of the fairy tale wish-fulfillment dream she was having and cringe. Before I could haul off after them, a sound from behind us made us turn.

"Sara Slick. By order of the *Pax Philosophia*, you are under arrest."

I knew that voice. Guild Agents.

"Shit," I exclaimed while turning and backing up to the boxes the Fae had been standing in front of. Ally nearly crawled up my arm, and I worried her poor heart couldn't handle the disappointment of the Fae being less than a cartoon film with sleeping princesses and getting tossed in jail on the same day.

"You need to come with us, Sara." Bentham spoke in an even, almost measured tone as if she'd rehearsed it. If you listened closely, there was empathy there, hidden behind layers of procedures, duty, and hierarchy. Bentham was one of the Guild's Agents who'd been chasing me for a while and seemed to at least be willing to give me the benefit of the doubt that I wasn't guilty. Her partner Thrash, on the other hand, either didn't have that room to believe or didn't care to. He wanted blood—specifically, mine.

Thrash had filed in behind her, and several other

Philosophers had entered the tent, too. Heavies. Goombahs meant to take me in if I started fighting, which I would. So, got me there, I guess.

"You guys know I'm innocent," I pressed while trying to ignore Thrash's scoff as he paced back and forth. "The real bad guy is Hobbes. I'm trying to help. Let me help."

"You stupid…" Thrash began, but Bentham interrupted him.

"My job," she cut in and glared at him. He backed off a little, but kept pacing, "is to bring you in, Sara Slick. My job isn't to judge your actions, past or present. My job is to bring you in and let the Guild do that. Period."

Ally had taken another step backward. I thought she was trying to get behind me. Out of the corner of my eye, I noticed what she was actually doing. The boxes were full of fireworks. And Ally still had the lighter.

Think fast, Slick.

"Okay. I didn't want to resort to this. But you guys forced me." I snapped the compass out of my pocket and pointed it at them like a weapon.

"Get down," Bentham shouted at the group, and they all hit the deck. She reached out, prepared to use a magic blast. I scanned the room with my stupid, temperamental compass.

"This," I bellowed, my voice full of action hero confidence, "is a sonic…uh, rune. It's capable of taking out all of you in one blast. Latest in rune technology. Cutting edge. Super powerful. So, if everyone can chill the hell out for a second."

I didn't know if they'd buy my lie, but they didn't move.

Looked like Archie's reputation as a runemaker had increased.

"You can't take on all of us," Thrash growled.

"Try me," I snapped back. "Ally?"

"Yeah?"

"When will..." I started.

"Oh, now-ish," she answered as she threw one of the fireworks at the Philosophers. It exploded in a shower of light, and we ran as fireworks exploded all around us, blowing up full boxes as we booked it for the other end of the tent and out into an increasingly confused parade, now suddenly featuring fireworks.

CHAPTER THREE

We barreled through the parade, did our best not to knock over any more stilt walkers, temporarily joined a float of flamboyant line dancers to make it to the other side, then ducked down a side street and got the parking lot within our sights. I looked back to see if we were being tailed and didn't see anyone, but I wasn't about to take anything for granted. Instead of running through the open area to the parking lot, I grabbed Ally by the elbow and ducked behind a tent, then wove our way toward a parking deck.

"We didn't park in there," Ally protested through labored breaths. I was running at nearly top speed, and despite being in good shape, Ally was struggling to keep up.

"I know, but come on."

We ducked into the parking deck and ran to the back, which led out to the parking lot itself but had an unobstructed view through a tinted window of the festival's exit. Ally crumpled against the wall, exhausted, while I scanned for any signs of the Philosophers. When none came after a few moments of silence, other than Ally's breathing, I sighed in relief and leaned against the wall.

"I think we lost them."

"Good, that's great. Shouldn't we go now?"

Something in my pocket vibrated, and since I saw Splinter poking his head out of Ally's jacket with tomato sauce on his lips, I knew it had to be the compass rune. I pulled it out to look at it. The finger was moving again, but was smooth and measured like it was tracking something. Despite the adrenaline and exhaustion, I couldn't quit now. We'd been dry on leads for a long time, and although this turned out to be a trap, I was desperate to eke out a win. These Fae might still know something.

"Not yet. We need some information, and I think I know how to get it."

"Don't we have all the information you need? The Fae creatures are causing havoc, and they lured you into a trap set by Philosophers. That's already a lot."

"More than that." I opened a soda and reveled in the sound of the aluminum top cracking. I took a giant gulp and shuddered as the carbonation hit hard, and memories of much better days zoomed through my mind at light speed. "Plus, I don't like being tricked."

I walked toward the end of the parking lot where the finger had pointed, and Ally groaned as she stood to follow. As we rounded a column, I heard voices in the distance and ducked, pulling Ally down behind a car with me when I saw the figure the voice belonged to. It was the leader of the Fae pack. She was speaking in giggling tones, delighted that her ruse had worked. The laughter in her voice made me angrier, and I touched my power-up rune, a locket around my neck. I did this fairly often, like a nervous tick. As long as I could touch it, I knew I had an ace in my pocket. It was still there. All I had to do was acti-vate it.

"Ally?"

"Yes?"

"Stay here."

"No problem," she responded.

I stood and activated the rune, opening the locket and letting the blue light pour out, then I snuck up on the Fae by ducking behind cars and rounding them to the side where none of them were actively looking. When I was close enough, I reached out and grabbed the leader, pulling her down and smacking her head into the concrete.

I dove out toward the other two, and one took off running. The other tried to swing a fist, but I ducked it and threw a punch to its gut that doubled it over. Even bent at the waist, it was nearly as tall as I was. I quickly stood, raised my knee and smashed it in its pretty face, and sent it buckling to the ground. Before I could turn around, the Fae's leader had kicked my back, and I sprawled forward before rolling to my feet and spinning to face her. The other Fae got to his feet and took off as well, leaving only the leader and me.

"Naida, let's go," one of them shouted as they ran.

Naida had no intention of leaving. She wanted the fight, and I was damn well going to give it to her. She rushed me with incredible speed, and I ducked out of the way barely in time. The Fae had long, powerful legs, which gave them one hell of a leap, and I narrowly escaped her fist before it crashed into me. Instead, it crashed through the side window of a car nearby, and I jumped to land a kick to her jaw. She staggered back, wrenching her arm from the window. Little rivulets of dark blood streamed from her lacerated flesh. I jumped at her again, but she caught me with her good arm in mid-air and slammed me down on the hood.

I tried to gain my breath as she stepped away while holding her arm and wincing. It took a lot to hurt a Fae but letting them hurt themselves was often the best way of causing damage. Now I had a target if I could get myself up and at her again. I rolled off the hood and stood across from her. She took off back toward the party without warning, and I chased after her.

"Come on," I shouted to Ally as we passed her, and with a groan, she joined the chase.

The Fae got as far as an empty dunking booth before I caught up with her, thanks to my rune and her energy waning due to blood loss. I tackled her and struggled with her until I had her bent over a giant bucket next to the booth, filled with water, apples, and the germs of a thousand drunken South Carolinians.

"You're going to talk to me," I shouted before dunking Naida's head into the water. When I pull her back up by the hair, she spat a stream of water into the air, then onto my face. I dunked her head again out of principle.

"I'd rather die a thousand deaths," she trilled when she came up. I dunked her again, this time forcing her to stay down a little longer. When I pulled her back up, she seemed less combative.

"I mean, I can kill you a thousand times over, won't bother me a bit. But I'd rather not spend my day doing this when I could eat funnel cake. How did the Philosophers find me, Naida? What do you know about Hobbes? The Harbingers?"

"I don't know any—" she began, and I dunked her head in again. When I felt like she might have gotten the point, I pulled her back up.

"What was that?" I asked.

"Fine! Fine," she sputtered, "they made us do it."

"Who?" I demanded.

"The Philosophers. They wanted to take you in, and they threatened us. Thrash, I think. He was going to arrest us for mixing with humans. We *like* humans. You're so funny when you're scared."

"What about the merpeople? Was that you?" I already knew the answer. Still, getting her talking might shake some information loose, if she had any to give.

"That was all me. Humans love mermaids. And they're always *so horny*. It's so easy to trick them into coming with us."

"What do you know about Hobbes? Where is he? What about the manifesto?" I demanded while holding her face above the water.

"I don't know! I don't care! It doesn't concern us, and I hate the politics. I simply want to be left alone," she screamed.

"So you can trick humans and scare them to death?"

"I was only having fun," she whined.

I sighed. I wouldn't get anything else out of Naida, and I knew it. Any further torture was purely for revenge, and frankly, I was too hungry to think about all these apples going to waste. They could have been pie.

"Fine, get out of here. Don't come back." I let the Fae up. As she stood, she looked around as if worried that a Philosopher was standing nearby and would punish her right then and there. When none came, she bared her teeth at me, hissed, and took off in the direction the other two had gone. I sat heavily on the dunking booth platform, and Ally walked up beside me.

"Well, that was a big old waste of time." She hopped up to sit beside me. Splinter shuffled out of her jacket, apparently full of whatever stolen items he had come across and hidden there, and crawled into my lap. I stroked his little head as I thought.

"Well, it might not have been a total waste," I finally responded.

"How's that?"

"No merpeople. That means it's taco time."

"Yeah, but we have Agents after us, don't we?"

"Yes, but after all these fake-mermaid people, I could *really* go for a fish taco."

"I'm not sure about the cause-and-effect relationship in your logic, but I'll go with it."

CHAPTER FOUR

After the incident at the festival, Ally and I decided it was time to regroup. We needed to head back to Archie's house, still without a clear idea of what to do once we left Charleston. The lack of leads was infuriating and kept us tied to the last place we knew the Harbingers were operating.

Plus, this was one of the few places where Archie had a local network of Runestuff dealers he could trust, making it our best place to hunker down for a while. Nevertheless, the ambush at the festival meant we were tempting fate the longer we stayed.

We headed to Archie's house and walked straight inside. The cool air from the window unit AC hit me as soon as the door opened, and was a welcome respite from the late summer heat outside. I closed my eyes momentarily while I let it unstick my clothes from my wet skin.

A string of profanity as creatively woven as it was nonsensical drifted up the steps toward us, and I opened my eyes. He sounded furious, and my stomach felt a little uneasy as I wondered if someone had found him. I rushed to the bottom of the steps and ran into the lab, and found him giving his lab table what-for.

Archie stood at the edge of the table, spewing swears at it like it had called him fat and offended his mama. I watched him for a few seconds while waiting for him to notice that we stood there, but he kept right on sputtering. I took another step toward him and realized he was working on something. On my next step, there was a minor explosion and Archie stumbled back. The front of his shirt smoked slightly and the hair at the edges of his face had singed, but he didn't seem too badly damaged by the whole situation.

"I don't want that rune." I crossed the room toward another table.

Archie whipped around to face me. "Slick. Ally. When did you two get here?"

"While you cursed that table up, down, sideways, and diagonally," I told him. "Seems it got the last word, though."

He threw a glance at the table and a small pile of still-sizzling debris sitting in the middle. "We'll see about that."

I set the bags in my hands on the table and unloaded them. "Come on over here and eat, and we'll tell you about the festival."

"Oooh, the festival. Sounds promising. What did you get to eat?"

"Tacos."

He dropped his head back and let out a groan. "Oh, for the love of..." Out of the corner of my eye, I saw Ally shoot him a threatening glare. His head popped up to give me a forced grin. "Delightful. Can't get enough of them."

I was still on my quest to try every type of taco that existed within my general vicinity. Over the several weeks that had passed since the showdown with the Philosophers and the massive bag of 'Celebration Taco Bell,' I had sampled far more tacos than I ever knew people had created. But there were always so many more to try, then add to my ever-growing chart of comparisons. One of these days, I'd crunch all the data to declare taco supremacy. Until then, I'd eat my way through them and make up for the lost time in The Deep.

"Great. Well, this one should be a special treat." I slid him a paper-wrapped taco.

Archie opened it and brought the soft tortilla-wrapped meat to his lips. "What is it?"

"Beef tongue with adobo sauce."

He made a face at me, his lips and nose seeming to crawl backward like they were trying to avoid the food I'd described. Archie braced himself and took a bite, anyway. I followed suit and chomped into my taco. He survived the first bite and continued his way through it. Apparently, beef tongue wasn't as horrific as he expected. I thought it was delicious. Not that I had a ton of experience with tongue of any kind, but it was certainly among my favorites.

"So, tell me about this festival," he said. "Did you get your hands on any of the merpeople?"

I shook my head as I wiped my mouth. "No. We didn't run into any of them, but we had the unique opportunity to beat the snot out of some Fae."

"Well, that's always fun. What were they doing at the festival?"

"That's where things get interesting. Apparently, the Philosophers sent them. There were never any merpeople to begin with. Only obnoxious little Fae running around scaring the living hell out of people. According to them, they didn't have any real information on Hobbes, only that they were sent to lay a trap. So, call me if you want to do a quick replay evaluation of the progress we've made. If you count everything we've learned over the last few weeks and the festival, we've gotten exactly nowhere."

"That's not entirely accurate," Archie objected.

"Really? Where exactly have we gotten?"

"You've learned a lot about tacos." He'd obviously been unprepared for me to challenge his optimism.

"That's true," I conceded. "But that won't do us a lot of good when it comes to the Harbingers. They're still operating. We know they're doing something, but we can't figure out what. So, either they're getting smarter, or they're planning something huge. All I know is, I haven't made any progress in tracking them down."

"Still no luck figuring out Hobbes?" Archie finished his taco and reached for another one. The tongue had grown on him.

"No."

"What do we know about him?" Ally asked.

"That his name is Hobbes," I said.

"Oh."

"Yeah. It's the minor little details we're missing, like who he is, why he's doing this, and why he framed me for a disgusting mass murder."

"Technically, it was your dad he framed."

I rolled my eyes at Ally. She shrugged. "What? It's the

truth. No way Hobbes could have foreseen you volunteering as tribute or whatever to save your dad."

I sighed, not wanting to continue with that line of thought. She was right, but more often than not, talking about my family filled me with emotions I didn't have time to deal with. I knew they were safe—Ally gave me weekly updates on their wellbeing—but the fact that my presence back in The Near put them at risk meant I couldn't see them. I had to focus on saving the world. The family reunion would be my reward only after I succeeded.

"Right now, I'm more concerned about the Philosophers pulling that trap. It means they're closing in," Archie said.

"I can handle it. There's nothing else I can do." I dropped the taco in my hands and wiped the juice from my fingers while letting out an exasperated growl. "Unless there's a special rune you have tucked away somewhere that will let me suck up all the Farsider scum and keep them in little tubes *Ghostbusters*-style. That's something I could appreciate."

Archie narrowed his eyes at me. "Hey. Not all Farsiders are assholes like the Fae. Some are like everybody else, trying to make it in the world."

He sounded offended, but I wasn't convinced. "Solon always said the same thing, and I was willing to buy it in The Deep. Magical prison isn't exactly a fair sample size. But my experience since coming back to Earth calls BS on your 'hashtag, not all Farsiders' nonsense. Almost every single non-human I've ever met wants me dead. The smart move is to assume they're all evil and act accordingly."

He shrugged. "I'm a Farsider, and you keep coming back to me."

Ally cocked her head at him, her huge dark eyes roving over his face and considering him as she chewed slowly. She had foregone the tongue. In her mouth was boring old chicken. "Why are you so different?"

He shrugged again. "There are almost no Farfolk born in The Heights. I was born here. After Pan'Rhea, most Farsiders were. Like them, I was born into hiding. We have to make our way in a world that isn't quite our home, surrounded by those who don't understand us. It isn't easy. And humans don't make it any easier."

"Humans have a right to defend themselves," I argued.

"Farsiders do, too. It's not like it was our choice to come here. The *Pax Philosophia* applies to us, as well."

I backed off, wanting to enjoy my tacos in peace rather than letting the conversation get any more heated. A little while later, I balled up the trash from lunch.

"We'll leave you to your work," I told Archie. "Be nice to the table for the rest of the day. You gave it a hard time there."

Ally and I left his house and walked through the city, our pace slow as we savored the moments of not being chased by anything that wanted to eat us.

"I can't believe I forgot to tell you this. You know who I saw the other day?" Ally asked.

"Me?"

"No. Well, yes. But other than that?"

"Who?"

"Anthony Rodriguez." Her voice reached a higher note that made me feel like we were back in high school.

"Really?" I sighed. "He's gorgeous." I straightened and looked at her questioningly when I realized it had been ten years since I saw the man, and a lot could have happened to diminish his appeal. Aging was less than kind to some people. "*Was* gorgeous?"

"Still is," she confirmed. "He mentioned you."

My eyes widened. "He did not! What did you say?"

Ally tilted her head at me while narrowing her eyes. "That I missed you dearly, and it was tough going these ten years without my best friend who disappeared from her living room never to be seen or heard from again."

"Oh." We walked a few more steps. "Bummer."

She shrugged. "It happens."

We rounded a corner, and I nearly knocked Ally down by sticking my arm out to stop her. In front of us was a group of punks, probably in their mid- to late-twenties, circling someone that they were taunting. I tried to hear what they were saying, but their words only came to me in snippets of the brutish, vulgar variety. Whoever they were circling was smaller than them and likely not prepared to fight off what looked like six average-sized meathead morons.

"You're not going to get in the mid—" Ally began, but I was already marching my way toward them. "Of course you are. Because, hey, six to one is good odds when you're completely insane."

"Hey, asshats," I shouted at the group, but they didn't seem to hear me over their game of 'make someone feel like shit.' "I said, hey, asshats!"

That time I caught one of their attention, and he smirked at me before going back to his fun. He slapped one of his friends on the shoulder and pointed at me. The friend looked up, his wide, dumb face red with rage.

"Who the hell are you?" Venom laced his voice, and spittle fell from the corner of his perennially downturned mouth.

"Leave him alone," I demanded as I got within feet of them.

"Fuck you," said the one closest and turned to shove me. That was exceptionally poor planning.

I snapped him over in a hip toss, using his momentum against him, and when he hit the ground, I twisted the arm I hadn't yet released and heard an audible snap from his shoulder area. His sudden scream of anguish at his now-broken arm drowned out his initial girlish scream of surprise.

A hand tried to grab my shoulder to spin me around, and I obliged by spinning much faster than the person intended and bringing my fist with it. I connected with his nose, crushing it back into the skull and sending a stream of snot-filled blood into the air and down his face. He stumbled backward while I kicked one of his buddies in the gut. He crumpled to the ground on one knee, and I stepped on his upright one to get some height to land a blow to the chin of one of the other jackasses.

They scattered. Three ran in the direction of the main street, around a corner, and off to wherever they had come from. Another ran past Ally, who surreptitiously tripped him. He scrambled back to his feet to run some more and rounded the corner we'd come from. That left Broken Arm McGee and Captain Flatnose.

Before I could do anything else, I caught sight of

Splinter crawling up the back of Flatnose's leg. Flatnose was now advancing on me, his jaw set in the way that goons since the caveman days have done to indicate that they intend to pound whatever they're looking at into submission. As he came within prime punching range, his body locked up and his mouth opened. No words came out, but his jaw flapped a couple of times like it wanted to. Then suddenly, he screamed...and screamed and screamed and screamed.

Then, Flatnose crumpled to the ground while thwacking his body in various places and keeping his legs together. Splinter dove out of the man's pants leg and bounded over to me. When he saw Splinter, Flatnose's eyes grew wide, and he stood to run but hobbled and kept his thighs tight.

"I don't want to know where you bit him, do I?" I asked Splinter as he wiggled his way back into my pocket.

"Thank you," came a voice from the middle of where the circle had been. I looked down and saw a Farsider kid. He looked vaguely human, but there was a gnomish quality to his cherub cheeks and short stature. It would explain the bullying. Even if they didn't know why those punks could tell this kid was different. I tried to push Archie's words out of my mind as I reached out.

Suddenly, the Farsider's eyes widened, and he backed up to the storefront of the building nearest him. "You. You're...you're Sara Slick!"

With that he took off, running for all he was worth and only looking back once when he rounded a corner and disappeared.

"You're welcome," I called after him.

"You have such a wonderful reputation, Slick. That kid was scared shitless of you," Ally joked. I didn't laugh.

"The only way to get the world not to hate me is to find Hobbes and prove my innocence." I eyed Broken Arm McGee.

"Then that's what we'll do. Together." Ally put her arm around my shoulder. I leaned my head in to touch hers and sighed.

CHAPTER FIVE

Splinter wasn't a big creature. He was small enough to take up residence in my pocket and be quite happy about it. But, the spiky little guy snored like a sailor three days into shore leave. Or my Great-Auntie Birdie. Nobody wanted to share their room with Great-Auntie Birdie when she visited for Thanksgiving.

My rodent companion was in full-on Macy's Day Parade turkey-induced snoring beside me on our hotel room bed, but I couldn't sleep. The room around me had come to feel like home. After spending so many years stuffed into cells with countless other people, grimy dangerous creatures, and the occasional corpse I talked to until it became a skeleton, the solitude was a luxury.

It didn't feel as much like a luxury that night. It felt like straight up being alone. No matter how much I tried to close my eyes and force myself to rest, my brain wouldn't let me. The events of the day looped through my mind like a torturous middle school mixtape created by a particularly uncreative ex-boyfriend.

Your heart simply cannot go on that long, Adam.

I couldn't stop thinking about the way the Farsider kid looked at me. It wasn't the same intimidation that younger people have on their faces when they look at an adult who's angry with them. It wasn't even the startled reaction of a boy who couldn't possibly imagine a girl laying the smackdown on him. He wasn't upset because of my one-woman anti-bullying campaign that saved his ass or that I proved to him his fighting skills weren't as impressive as he wanted to think they were.

The look in his eyes was sheer terror. He knew who I was, and was deeply, intensely afraid of me.

There was a time when I wouldn't have gotten anywhere near that type of reaction. I wasn't the one inspiring fear. Instead, I was the one suffering it every moment of every day. I could still so distinctly remember my first days in The Deep. The hopelessness and helplessness of not understanding why I was there and fully believing those dirty, miserable walls would be where I died made me feel hollow. The only thing that saved me from imploding and giving into the darkness was Solon.

The powerful wizard didn't teach me not to be afraid. That's not something he could have taught. Instead, he taught me to take that fear and not run away from it. He taught me to turn it into myself and use it to protect and fuel me. That fear told me when I needed to act. It told me when I needed to push back against it and force it behind me.

Then Solon taught me to kill. I would never forget those first kills. Never in my life would I have imagined being a person who would take the life of another living creature. I scooped up spiders and brought them outside and opened windows for flies. But there came a time when I no longer had the option for compassion.

It was my life or theirs, and I was going to win every single time. That's when I knew I still had fight in me. The first time I was able to look into the eyes of another inmate and tear his belly open with the switchblade I took from Solon's hand, I knew somewhere deep within me there was still value and drive. I hadn't given up yet.

But those eyes were still with me. Bloodshot and wild, they stared back at me from the scarred face of a battle-torn goblin who knew nothing but blood and torment. They met me with a threat. But as soon as the lifeblood poured across my hand and spilled out onto the floor, that threat became a plea, then a release. I wanted to think after that first death I wouldn't be afraid, but that wasn't the case. More deaths, more fear, more eyes. The eyes always stayed with me. Sometimes they held anger and hatred until the very last second. Other times, they almost seemed grateful.

It was terrifying, then. That world was nothing but horror and clawing to stay alive. In this world, I was the terrifying one.

That was a lot to process. As I tried to think it through, I toyed with the locket Solon gave me. My fingers flipped and twirled it on my chest and occasionally picked it up so I could look at it. It was one of the most important possessions I'd ever had in my life. Not only because of how many times since he gave it to me that it'd saved me, but also the link it gave me to my mentor.

Having the rune made me feel like I still had Solon

close to me. It still hurt so much that he was gone. There were moments when I almost turned to talk to him or tried to call for him so I could ask for his help. In the instant's flash it took for the realization to settle in, the pain was always fresh. It was like I had watched my trusted friend die again.

But this rune carried me through. It reminded me of the darkest moments of my existence when Solon still saw light. Even when I was sprawled on the ground, waiting for the next assault to finally finish me off so I could join the blood splatters on the stone and the bones in the pit, he saw more.

It wasn't an accident that he saved me that night. He chose to. He could have left me to get tossed around like a volleyball by the giantess, spooky marshmallow spider, and goblin with mommy issues, then eaten as their midnight snack. He didn't. He saved me and kept saving me.

And the rune kept me going. There had been so many times when I was right on the brink of disaster, and this little creation pulled me right back to save my ass. I wondered if he knew that would happen, if he gave me the rune as a source of comfort and a precaution, or if he could look ahead and see the challenges I'd face. One conversation we had reverberated in my mind.

After one of the fiercest fights I ever had to endure within the walls of The Deep, he sat with me in the cell. We sat there in silence for several long minutes. Both of us saw the guards lurking in the back of the gathered crowd as I thrashed and flailed with the cyclops. They watched with as much sickening delight as the other inmates.

It was a sinking moment for me. I already knew I was

screwed. That wasn't something that could miss my awareness after more than about two hours in The Deep. But seeing the guards like that reinforced how dark my future was. Finally, he turned to me.

"One day, I won't be here. One day, you'll be on your own. Trust yourself as much as you trust me. Because I do."

I tried not to disturb Splinter as I climbed off the slightly damp, sagging bed. The careful effort was wasted. He flopped over into the indentation I left and kept right on snoring. I made my way over to the window, then moved the curtains aside and looked out over the parking lot.

I wasn't really alone. Out in the shadows, I saw Dog marching paces around the hotel. I didn't know what he was doing there, but it wasn't the first time he'd shown up. Over the last several weeks, he'd shown up a handful of times and did the exact same thing. He paced around the hotel for hours, never wavering in his path or making any effort to communicate with me.

He believed me when I told him his pack's deaths weren't at my hands. At least, I thought he did. He seemed to recognize my innocence and know I was being framed. But I still hated that his life was destroyed and somehow, although I didn't know how, I was connected to it.

There was only one option in front of me. If I wanted to help Dog and myself, I had to find the real heinous one. And that meant finding Hobbes.

CHAPTER SIX

I finally fell asleep at some point during the night and woke up to the sound of Splinter munching his way through a bag of Cheese Doodles on the dresser. It wasn't one of those piddly little individual packets that barely had more than a handful. I'd gone for the full family size, and Splinter had established himself as his very own family.

Almost his entire body was inside the bag. Only his chubby little rodent butt stuck out of the opening. Streaks of unnatural, vibrant orange cheese powder clung to his spikes. It was a good look for him. A little punk makeover to give him some extra edge. He wriggled backward and looked over at me.

"Started breakfast without me?"

His whiskers twitched as he considered what I said. He delved back into the bag and came out with one of the doodles in his mouth. He threw himself off the dresser and landed on the comforter beside me, then scrambled up to me to offer the crunchy snack. He was such a good listener.

"Thank you." I took it from him and popped it into my mouth. "Grab me another one."

I held my hand out to show him it was empty, helping him understand what I said. He scurried away and came back with another. I was taking it out of his mouth when the door to my room opened and Ally walked in. She cringed when she saw me take the doodle and bite through it.

"You did not just eat something out of his mouth."

"Yes, I did. Why not?"

She closed the door and gave the slight shudder she always did when entering my room. In her defense, she was doing better with it. She willingly came inside and lingered for longer than a few seconds now. That was saying a lot for her. It still felt like a palace to me.

"Because he's a rodent?" she asked.

"Not a good enough reason for me. Splinter and I go way back. I'll share food with him any time." I reached to scratch his head, and he nuzzled me happily.

"Brought your clothes." She held up the black duffel bag she brought with her every day.

It was her concession to my choice of living arrangements. She agreed I could stay in the hotel as long as I didn't smell like the hotel. I thought that was fair. The lingering damp odor was less noticeable after spending hours in the room, but it stood out when it hung out in my clothing fibers.

After accepting the bag from her, I swapped the clothes inside for the ones I was wearing, then tucked the dirty clothes into the pack so Ally could wash them. It was like a strange drug exchange.

"So, what's the play? What's on tap for today?"

I stared at her questioningly. "How do you possibly take the time for this? For me?"

My best friend laughed. "This is my job. I'm researching, getting ready for the big scoop."

"What big scoop?" I perched on the edge of the dresser to tie my boots.

Splinter noticed me getting ready and rushed back to the bag, stuffing his cheeks full of doodles for the road.

"The online news site I work for has a little clout. They're throwing me a few dollars to investigate. Plenty of folks are on total bullshit assignments, and I convinced the editor that this is worth the wondrously low pay I've been getting," Ally told me.

I looked back at her in confusion. We'd had this discussion several times already, but the economics of it still seemed weird. "I still don't really understand."

"I told you. I work for an online news site," Ally told me. "It's one of the more high-end ones, which is why I finagled getting paid to traipse around with my best friend going after the bad guys under the guise of writing a story. In fact, I might *actually* write the story. With your identity properly protected, of course."

"High-end news site? Like MySpace?"

Ally laughed and shook her head. "Everything's changed, Slick. MySpace isn't really a thing anymore. Well, it is, but not like you remember. Now, it's mostly a bunch of shitty amateur bands trying to make themselves seem legit."

I stared at her while blinking a few times. "No more MySpace? But mine was so carefully cultivated."

"I know. Your intro music game was on point," Ally confirmed. "Things have moved on."

"But what about my Top Eight?" I felt surprisingly emotional about mourning the end of my high school social media attachments.

"It might still exist in cyberspace somewhere, but you should let it go. I'll teach you all about the new stuff," Ally promised.

"You'll always be Top Eight in my heart," I told her.

She laughed and opened her arms to hug me. "You too, Slick."

"All right, so you work for an online news site, and they're paying you to investigate what's going on," I recapped.

"Right. Which means I basically have all the time in the world for this. Everything we do falls under the umbrella of research. I'm getting paid to run around with you, and there's nothing they can do about it because they authorized a story on potential supernatural links to the kidnappings. They can't argue with me pursuing the supernatural angle."

"No, they can't. Do you make enough money doing that?"

"Enough. Not a lot. I wouldn't say they pay me well or anything, but it's enough if I live cheaply. That's not too difficult since it's only me."

"Silver linings."

"So, I came here to ask you what your plan is for the day."

"I know. You already did. But I don't really have one. I mean, it's the same basic plan we always have. Figure out how to take Hobbes down. That's kind of my overarching theme at this particular juncture in my life."

"It's your brand."

"I don't know what that means."

"Never mind. But you don't have any particular direction for today?"

"No."

"Good. Because all my discretionary time has revealed a lead for us. Something that might have something to do with The Far."

She sounded delighted, but I was cautious. "What do you mean?"

Ally perched on the dresser and settled into place. She had yet to sit on any of the soft surfaces of the room. That day might come. I doubted it, but it might.

"I did some research and found out there's a shipping company on the north side of town that's cooking their books."

"And how did you find that out?" It never ceased to amaze me how she stumbled on her leads.

"Combination of websites, but mostly Reddit." I opened my mouth, but before I could ask, she shoved one finger in the air and shook her head. "It will be a part of your contemporary internet survival skills seminar."

"Okay. What does that mean for us?"

"It's unclear what they're shipping. The contents of their crates are...ambiguous."

"How ambiguous?"

"Enough to raise red flags."

I drew in a breath as the realization settled over me.

"Farside artifacts."

She nodded. "Maybe. It's not like we haven't seen that before."

My thoughts went back to the warehouse the day we met Archie. The Harbingers there were shipping artifacts. It was possible they were doing the same thing here. I stood and scooped Splinter into my hand.

"It's worth a look. Let's go."

CHAPTER SEVEN

"Where the hell did you go?" Ally asked as I climbed over the top of the ladder and back onto the rooftop. Since I was carrying a drink carrier, three bags, two apples, and a giant-sized bag of potato chips, I wasn't pleased with her attitude. But I let it pass. Ally got hangry often.

"I got you burgers." I waved the bag and walked toward her.

"Well, okay. No pickles, right?" she asked.

"I thought you liked pickles?"

"I do. I love them. But I'm trying a new non-green diet. Latest trend."

"But burgers are fine?" I was perplexed.

"Mmm-hmm," she agreed through a mouth full of hamburger, followed quickly by three fries at a time and a gulp of her soda.

"I think you missed something somewhere in that diet." I sat on the blanket we'd laid out for ourselves.

"What did you get?" Ally was now stuffing fries into her face by the fist-load.

"Tacos," we said in unison.

"Yup." I pulled out several of the silver foil-wrapped joyous meals of the gods.

We sat in silence for a few minutes, quietly munching away on what was our second meal of the day up here. Thus far, it had been boring as hell. Stakeouts weren't nearly as sexy as they seemed in the movies, although the fast food wrappers usually seen in the cop car were accurate, at least. Our now increasing pile of trash, currently being dug through by Splinter, sat on the edge of our blanket.

We had laid out the blanket near the edge of the roof, covering the hard concrete with the thinnest layer of soft cotton to save our knees a little. Our vantage point atop a nearby empty office building in the industrial area gave us a direct line of sight down to the warehouse. The cars came in from one direction and headed out another, but both went right by our building, and it gave us a good chance to see inside each one.

At first, it was almost like a picnic. We brought up drinks and sandwiches and mostly chatted while we kept a loose eye on the building across from us. The warehouse was a hive of activity, but it all seemed quite normal for a warehouse in this part of town. None of the packages seen going in or out looked suspicious, and I relegated myself to waiting around until dark.

That was when the shenanigans, if any, were likely to begin. Ally brought breakfast, so I volunteered to get the early dinner. After skipping lunch, and with Ally's infamous grumpiness if she had to sit still too long and also had to skip meals, I was more than willing to stretch my legs and make my way to the burger shack and the taco stand a few streets over. The likelihood I would miss anything was low, and besides, I wanted to get to that taco truck myself.

"So, how many trucks have you seen since I left?" I asked.

"I lost count." Ally suppressed a burp. She smiled sheepishly in the way she always had, although between us girls, I could out-burp any man walking on God's green Earth and she knew it. "Like, twenty, I'd say, but it's been regular. Every couple of minutes a crew goes out, checks the load, signs a paper, hands it to the driver, and off they go. Nothing abnormal."

That's what worried me. Something wasn't right about this place, but nothing seemed odd when it was examined. My watch said it was almost five, which meant they should be gearing up for a shift change soon. Maybe that would liven things up.

As dark fell, Ally got restless and started pacing on the roof. When the streetlights came on and the sun set over the horizon, I checked my watch again. Nine-thirty. If the night shift was up to something, they'd be doing it soon. This was getting dumb.

Finally, as my watch hit eleven-fifteen, a truck pulled up to the warehouse. It had been mostly silent since about six, with workers leaving and a bunch of vehicles arriving to be loaded but none leaving or arriving since around seven. The streetlights burned a bright yellow, but the light was dim by the time it reached the ground and it was difficult to see much of anything. But what I saw got me excited. The driver of the new truck was a Farsider.

He wore a disguise, but it was easy to tell he wasn't human, at least for me. A weird shuffle to his step indicated he either suffered from a terrible knee injury or hid a tail or something in his pants leg. Since he kept licking his lips with a tongue that would impress Gene Simmons, I was betting on the latter. I kicked Ally's shoes, but she didn't move. I tried again and got a grunt. She had fallen asleep again, the second time tonight. I kicked her shoe one last time.

"What, what?" She sat up and rubbed her eyes.

"Wake up, sleepybones. We got ourselves a Farsider. I need you to keep a lookout and wait here while I scope it out."

"Fine." She yawned and sipped her undoubtedly hot and stale soda. She grimaced and sat up fully, then placed her elbows on the roof of the building and looked down at the warehouse. "I can barely see anything," she said to my back as I walked to the ladder.

"Good." I hopped on. "Maybe they won't see me, either."

I looked down at the locket out of habit again, ensuring that it was fully charged. If I got my ass kicked by whatever was in that warehouse, the rune inside the locket would refill my energy and then some. I would be incredibly powerful for a short burst, but then it would zap out of me. It had come in handy before, and I needed to make sure I could use it again any time I did something where I might be outnumbered.

I slid down the rungs and onto the street and took off for the warehouse. It was surprising how dark it seemed despite the light of the streetlamps. As I stood in the shadows, I felt like I might be invisible in the darkness. I found my way to the back of the building and spotted where a door stood cracked open. While sneaking my way closer, I noticed that it seemed empty and there were no lights on. I slid my way inside and crept behind some boxes until I felt like I was about halfway into the spacious room.

Suddenly, there was light everywhere. I spun around to gain my bearings and noticed that I was in a large room, surrounded by crates, and much to my dismay, about a dozen Philosophers. They made their way toward me in the 'sort of hurrying, but too cool to run' way that Guild Agents tended to use when they felt like they had you trapped. Which, currently, they did.

Shit.

Bentham and Thrash came from behind them. Thrash held Ally, one hand over her mouth, and Bentham looked like she had stepped in the world's largest turd. Ally looked like she might be in pain, and I stepped toward her.

Bentham held up her hand to stop me. "No, Slick. Not one more step."

"Let her go." My eyes bored holes into Thrash.

"You're becoming predictable, Slick," Bentham continued, undeterred. "I barely put any thought into this little ruse, and yet, here you are. We waited for you to come down and into the warehouse for *hours*. For a moment, I thought you had us figured out. It's almost a shame you didn't. I thought higher of your intelligence, and Thrash was itching for a chase. I simply wanted you contained in the warehouse so you couldn't cause us more trouble."

"It's not as much fun when you don't know we're coming." Thrash snickered. "I like it when I can smell fear."

"No one else likes that they can smell you," I retorted.

Thrash bared his teeth and seemed to shift Ally around, causing her to moan in pain. I winced.

"Your sarcasm isn't doing your friend any favors, Slick."

I shifted my focus to Bentham. "Let her go, and I won't have to use this." I touched the locket and held it in front of me. Bentham scoffed and looked at Thrash, who shook his head.

"I'm not scared by a silly compass. You might have tricked me last time, Slick, but this time, I got you."

This was going to suck. I had no choice, though. Bentham brought this on herself. The locket was fully charged, but I was way outnumbered. This locket had slowly given me extra strength for years, but I needed more. It was literally the only shot I had at taking them all down, at least for long enough to escape, but I had to destroy it to use all the energy it held, rendering it useless afterward.

The thought of using all the power Solon gave me and relinquishing the locket I'd worn around my neck for so long gave me pause, but I had to push through. There was no other way. This is what he would have wanted.

"You seem to like me being predictable so you can do your job, isn't that right?" Bentham nodded and opened her mouth to say something, but I interrupted her. "You'll hate this, then."

I crushed the locket in my hand and destroyed the rune inside. My eyes welled with tears as power immediately surged into my palm, through my wrist, and into my veins. It pulsed through my body, filling me with an incredible sense of dominion over everything in my sight. Thoughts of Solon filled my mind, and I felt like I could do anything and bend reality to what I wanted it to be. And right now, I wanted to kick some ass.

Bentham's eyes grew wide as she backed up a step. Thrash's jaw went slack, and Ally tried to scream. Pure energy in light form shot from my body in all directions, and I went stiff with it. It poured out of my eyes and mouth and fingers. Anything in its way got zapped, flying backward and away from the light. It stopped bursting from me as suddenly as it came and instead hovered around the edge of me like a yellow aura that sizzled and cracked.

Philosophers came at me, but it was like fighting people who were underwater. I moved faster, hit harder, and took almost no damage. Time was slow but increasing in speed, getting me back to real-time. I knew it was only my perception of it while my body moved much faster than it should, but it felt like I moved normally and everyone else had hit the slo-mo button.

When I had incapacitated everyone else, I turned to Thrash. He tossed Ally to the floor and charged at me. His huge fist flew toward me but time still hadn't returned to full speed yet, so I ducked it easily, then jumped into an uppercut that sent him across the room like a cartoon. He crashed into several boxes and laid there unconscious. Bentham charged then. I ducked her, flipped her over my back, then kicked her in the middle of hers. She stumbled to the floor and turned, but met my knee in her jaw. She was out, and time had returned to normal speed.

I was slowing and knew that soon I would be exhausted. We needed to get out of here as fast as possible. I grabbed Ally and took off for the door, but I stole one look back as we crossed the threshold. Pieces of the rune that had been in the locket were strewn all over the floor. I'd shoved the rest of it in my pocket as I fought, but seeing those pieces there made me want to run back and get them. To gather up every speck of the rune Solon had given me. But I couldn't. I had to get myself and Ally to safety. I turned my head and looked out over the street. We were alone.

Good. Time to move.

CHAPTER EIGHT

Archie wasn't having any deep and meaningful conversations with the furniture in his lab when I got Ally back to it. That was a good thing. I wasn't in the mood to deal with any other elements of his lab exploding. I'd had my fill of nonsense and was seething when I got her down the stairs and to the cot set up against the wall.

That little bed had seen a lot in the last couple of months. Any time any of us sustained injuries while out pursuing Hobbes and the Harbingers, this was where we ended up. Fortunately, most of those injuries were minor and required only a little patching up to manage.

That was the case now. It was Ally's turn to stretch out across the cot and let us check her over for damage. She was a little beat up, nothing too severe, but that didn't temper how I felt. I was pissed. It infuriated me to see her hurt because she was doing everything she could to help me. Being in that position at all only made it worse. It shouldn't have unfolded like that. We should have been able to go to the warehouse and find out more about it without an ambush.

Bentham was too good. She knew too much and was nipping right at our heels.

"I'm sorry, Slick," Ally said. "Two traps in two days. I guess I'm not very good as a researcher."

"Shut up." I laughed. "Without your help, I have nothing. Except maybe dancing around in the middle of downtown, hoping Hobbes shows up to fight before the Philosophers Guild gets me. We're all learning on the go here."

"Yeah, but you're the one always paying for it."

"You don't get to say that while you're bleeding."

"It's fine. Only a few bumps and scratches. Nothing like the stuff you've been through. I'll be fine. I have to pick up some of your street cred at some point, don't I?"

She was teasing and laughing to make me feel better, but it wasn't working. I finished cleaning another scrape across her arm and smoothed an adhesive gauze pad over it.

"It's not fine. Maybe I'm too reckless."

"You've been doing what you have to do," Archie told me. "Like you said, the Harbingers are still working. We have to keep pushing if we're going to find Hobbes and stop him."

"I still haven't been careful enough. We can't stop looking for answers, but we also can't keep going like we have been. If we keep doing it this way, it will get us killed. Or worse, sent to The Deep. I know neither of you has had the distinct pleasure of camping out there, but I need you to accept my review. It is not somewhere you want to end up," I told them.

"You've been out of that place for a few months now. You've encountered the Harbingers a bunch of times. I haven't seen a fight affect you like this before. Are you upset only because they ambushed you at the warehouse?" Archie prodded.

I shook my head and reached into my pocket to pull out the remnants of the locket Solon made me. Seeing the broken shards in my palm made my throat tighten with emotion, and my eyes sting with tears made sharper with their blend of sadness and fury.

"I broke my locket." I carried the pieces over to him and tipped them into his cupped hands. "Do you think you could do anything with them?"

"Shit, Sara, I'm sorry. I'll do what I can, but Solon created something truly special. That was a sophisticated rune. I'm not sure if I can match that."

I nodded sadly and dropped to sit on a stool next to one of the tables. There had been a little hope left in me after destroying the locket. I did what I had to do, although it was devastating to do it. But there was a part of me that had hoped Archie might be able to save what was left. The uncertainty in his eyes as he looked down at the cracked and crumbled pieces of the rune didn't give me any confidence.

"Is there anything that might make you feel better?" Ally asked.

"I don't know. I can't think. That locket meant so much to me, Ally. Not only for the power it brought but for who gave it to me. I hate it. I hate it."

Her eyes brightened, and she slid to the edge of the cot. "Hey, do you remember when we were kids and my goldfish died? I was so upset because I'd had him for a long time, and he meant so much to me. You made me feel better."

I looked at her suspiciously. "Are you suggesting we hold a funeral for the leftover pieces of my rune and bury it in the backyard?"

"If it would make you feel better."

"Let's not go to those extremes yet," Archie told her. "Let me see what I can do with the fragments first. I can't guarantee anything, but I might be able to figure something out. And if not, then we can have a dignified burial for it."

Ally gave a single nod and reached over to rub my leg comfortingly. I sighed.

"Thanks." Splinter crawled onto my lap from where he'd perched at the end of the bed by Ally's feet. He stood on his back legs and pressed his front paws to my chest while rubbing his face against mine like a kitten. I ran my hand down his back and along his little arm flaps. "You know, today started with so much promise. Splinter stopped snoring long enough for me to get some sleep. We shared Cheese Doodles for breakfast. Then I find out MySpace has bit the big one, get ambushed during what I think will be a little recon, and destroy my locket, one right after the other."

We were silent for a few seconds. Then Ally perked up again. "I have an idea."

"I'll start working on the musical selections for the burial," I told her.

"Good, but that's not it. I think the best thing right now

would be for you to get out of town. Things are getting a little too tense around here," she suggested.

I looked over at her, intrigued by the idea. "You mean like a vacation?"

She shook her head. "Not exactly. A source got in touch with me saying he might have some information that might interest me. Now, I get weird emails all the time. You do enough paranormal and supernatural research and whacked-out people start crawling out of the woodwork wanting to tell you their story. I get messages every day from people telling me they've been abducted by aliens or had a tea party with Bigfoot. But I've spent enough time around you and your new friends to tell when someone has seen something."

"What do you have?"

"This guy contacted me from West Virginia. That's Woodbooger territory, so you know I get to hear all the craziness. But he wasn't rambling about any of that. He offered me some credible information about a weird cult living deep in the woods and possibly connected to recent murders. Do we know of any people who others might perceive as a weird cult and might enjoy murder-lurking around in the woods?"

I glanced at Archie, then back to Ally. "We may."

She laughed miserably. "With my recent track record, it's probably another one of Bentham's traps. But it might be worth checking out."

I thought about the offer. Getting out of The Deep put me into a world so unfamiliar to nearly everything I'd known. There was so much for me to learn and experience, but I'd spent the vast majority of my new freedom close to the same area. Now Ally was offering me the chance to keep doing what I needed to do to find Hobbes and stop him from completing his evil plan while also stretching out a little more. I nodded.

"A road trip sounds perfect."

CHAPTER NINE

"Convenience stores are amazing these days," I said to Ally as we explored the sprawling shop.

"You've been to rest stops before."

"Yeah, but nothing like this. When I went," I glanced around and noticed we were far from the only people in the store at the time. I leaned a little closer to her, "*away,* I was getting used to design-your-own sandwich shops in gas stations. Now it's a whole new world of road tripping. Did you see all this stuff?"

My arms were already overflowing with mounds of snacks as I rushed over to a frozen yogurt machine up against one wall. I pointed at it and gave an open-mouthed look of amazement to my best friend. She laughed and shook her head in amusement. I couldn't pass it up. After juggling all my other selections into one arm, I pulled a Styrofoam cup from the dispenser and pulled down the lever to distribute a perfect frosty swirl of chocolate and vanilla into the bottom. To my side was a toppings bar with dozens of options in little silver containers. I pored over them like I was making the biggest decision of my existence.

"What are you doing?" Ally walked up to my side.

"Trying to decide what topping to put on my frozen yogurt. What do you think? Crumbled up cream-filled chocolate cookies or tiny little M&M's?"

"It's unlimited toppings, Slick. You could have both."

I gasped. "Oh... my... God. I'm going to have both."

She could have left me happily standing there beside the toppings bar distributing sprinkles of cookies and candy over my frozen yogurt like some tremendously benevolent topping deity raining down on my itty-bitty yogurt people, and I probably would have considered the road trip a success. Ally, not so much. We still had a while to go to get to West Virginia, and she was eager to get back on the road. But the glow of the phenomenal convenience store had called to me. She could have kept right on driving past it if she wanted to. A sign a couple of miles back told us there were other options for stopping for gas, and I was positive somewhere along the line we could find a grimy little roadside bathroom should the need arise.

But, no. She stopped here, and now I was enraptured.

"I think your sandwich is ready," she told me. "The guy behind the counter has been waving the bag at you for the last thirty seconds."

"There's a number on my ticket. He could have called me."

"Number 6750? He did."

"Oh. He did."

I finished the flurry of embellishments atop my frozen yogurt and made my way over to the counter to accept my sandwich. It nestled in the white paper bag with two cups. One overflowed with beer-battered onion rings and the other with french fries. What a time to be alive. And not in prison.

"So, now you think you have everything you need?" Ally asked.

I nodded. "I'm pretty sure I'm good. This should carry me through the rest of the trip."

"I should hope so. It's only a couple more hours. I'll get gas while we're here and we shouldn't have to stop again. Unless all that hits you somewhere between here and there."

"Maybe there will be another one of these stores somewhere."

"Maybe there will be an open field you can squat in, so we don't take another hour and a half."

"You have no sense of adventure," I informed her.

"And you have no self-control. Put down the dog treat. We don't have a dog with us."

I thought about the massive black dog growling in the parking lot behind my hotel. I wondered how he would react to me not coming back for the next couple of days. But that wasn't the motivation behind me grabbing the adorable cupcake-shaped cookie.

"This is for Splinter," I told her. We headed for the cashier, and another display caught my eye. "Look at the miniature glasses of wine! I'm getting one." I snatched a glass from the display and looked at it happily.

"Why do you need a miniature glass of wine?" Ally asked.

"Because I turned twenty-one years ago and haven't had

a chance to buy any alcohol. I want to. It's my right as a grown adult."

"You don't have an ID."

"Damn it."

She snatched the glass from my hand and added it to the small assortment of snacks she'd chosen. "I'll use my ID to get it for you. But you're not allowed to get belligerent on me."

The snacks and gas were courtesy of Archie, who made good money on his black-market activities and stashed away most of it for a rainy day. Turned out, we were his rainy day. Right before we left, he took a stack of money out of a hidden compartment in the wall and handed it to us. It would supplement Ally's pay for our road trip and make it easier for us to get what we needed. It was an unexpected gesture, and one I was positive was directed right at Ally.

After pumping the gas, we were on our way. I sat in the passenger seat with my loot spread out around me, happily holding my glass of wine. I had no intention of opening it. It simply made me strangely happy to have it. Although I still hadn't technically bought alcohol since the man at the bar bought my beer and Ally bought my wine, it was still a little glimpse of adulthood.

"All right, so tell me more about this guy from the internet," I said after downing most of my sandwich and half the onion rings. The fries would come as a second course.

Until this point, our trip had been about listening to bad mixtapes and reminiscing about when we were younger. We'd always talked about taking long road trips when we were in college, but obviously, this was the first chance we had. Now it was time to buckle down and think about the reason we ventured out in the first place.

"I first found him on a message board. I have a list of them I cycle through every couple of days to catch up on the latest rumors, sightings, and stories. They're where I start a lot of my investigations. This guy's name is Jonas. We'd never interacted directly, but I'd seen his name pop up now and then. He emailed me because he'd seen my past reporting on weird phenomena. He thought I was the right one to help him."

"How flattering."

"Yep. I have a way with the guys. Lure them right in with my astounding connections to the strange and often distasteful."

"It's a special appeal."

"Well, Jonas was eager to get hold of me. But he didn't tell me much. All the messages said was there were these strangely brutal killings near an odd off-the-grid community. He wouldn't give any details or anything until we met in person. It was all vague, but it sounds like possible Farsider activity to me."

"They won't be able to hide for long with Slick and Ally on the case." I stuffed a handful of fries into my mouth.

"Let's hope."

Between us on the console, Splinter happily nibbled his way through the cupcake dog cookie. It was almost half as big as his body, but I had total faith he'd get through it by the time we got to West Virginia. He might sleep for a few days afterward, but that was fine. Ally reached into my lap to snitch some fries, then grinned at me as she turned back to the road.

We spent the next hour seeing if any of our favorite old dance moves could be effectively recreated in a sitting position and working our way through my mountain of snacks. Ally's beat-up old vehicle was the perfect choice for the trip, and I was enjoying being out experiencing new things. We were getting close when I saw a broken-down car on the side of the road ahead of us.

"Slick," Ally pointed it out. "We should stop and see if they need any help. It's the least we can do for our fellow man."

I sighed heavily. "Look at you, having all kinds of compassion."

"You could stand to learn some compassion too, Slick."

She pulled off a few yards behind the car and got out. I'd only taken a few steps toward the vehicle when something rustled loudly in bushes beside the road. I turned in time to see people climbing out of the bushes toward us. I instantly recognized the glittering wings and tall, thin bodies. They were Fae, and their 'too cool for this world' demeanor had vanished. They were ready for a fight.

It was a trap.

"Fucking compassion," I muttered.

CHAPTER TEN

I hopped over the hood of the car, sliding like a Duke boy, and landed on my feet ready to swing. The Fae kept back, obviously a little warier of my fighting skills now. Ally slammed my door shut, and I heard the automatic lock come from inside. I looked down into her window and saw her flash me a thumbs-up and a cheesy smile. I knew she would try to help me if it looked like I needed it, and frankly, I was glad she was out of the way and out of danger, but still. Rude.

"Get her," Naida screamed.

The first of the Fae tried to make a move. I dodged him, grabbed his wrist in mid-punch, and twisted his arm behind him. I swung him around in front of me in time for one of the Fae to accidentally punch him while aiming at me. The second Fae must have been damn strong because the wrist I held suddenly went limp and the Fae crumpled to the ground. The Fae leader stayed back and watched as the second Fae swung at me.

I ducked and slammed a fist into his stomach. His abs

were as hard as a rock, and I wasn't entirely sure I did any damage, but he buckled and fell back a step to gain his balance. Despite not having my locket anymore, I still had my training, and my fists and kicks found weak spots no matter how strong the enemy. As he stepped back, I leapt forward and kicked his chin. He fell to the ground dazed as the leader looked down at him in disgust.

"Perith, you idiot. This is why I brought backup," Naida said scornfully.

"Backup?" I questioned.

The leader smiled as two more Fae came from the wooded area beside us. Both were tall and gorgeous with long blonde hair falling in braids to their waists. Aside from the braided hair, they looked much like Naida. Unlike the men, the female Fae were a little smaller and more innocent-looking. The leader laughed as her two clone-like minions advanced on me. They smiled and showed off their needlelike teeth. Teeth that ripped what they ate to shreds.

"Silly Sara Slick," Naida mocked, "now you'll pay for embarrassing me!"

She shrieked as she too charged. I thought quickly and flipped out of the way, letting the other two stumble and trip over each other in an effort to turn and catch me. Instead, I went right for the source. A thrust kick directly into Naida's knee sent her barreling to the ground, smashing into the gravel hard, and slicing up her face. As she tried to stand, I field goal-kicked her head so hard I was pretty sure I broke a toe. It did the job, though, snapping her head back so sharply she instantly went unconscious.

The other two Fae were on me now, each trying to grab an arm. I wrestled one free and used it to punch one in the nose, and when they let go of my other arm, I elbowed the other in the stomach. With both hands free, I smashed their heads together.

They crumpled to the ground while shrieking at their bloody faces. That left Perith, who was now standing and looking down at his defeated brethren, and knew I did all that unassisted.

On my own. Without the locket. A pang of sadness coupled with rage filled me as I thought about Solon. I had lost so much of the life I should have had, and now I was losing parts of the life I *did* have.

I was highly trained even without the locket and kept myself in fighting shape at all times despite the taco gorges. But without it, I felt their hits a little more than usual. I felt bruises swelling under my skin as I stood there, and I was a little more winded than usual. I tried to brush it off, though, because while I might feel it, there was no reason for them to know that.

There was a tense moment where I thought Perith would run. Simply pick up and bolt the other way. But then he looked down and saw his leader, and something steeled inside him. He charged.

Dummy.

He threw several fists, and I dodged them all pretty well until the last one. That one landed hard on my jaw, and for a moment, I saw stars. It was enough time for him to grab me by my shirt and toss me on the roof of the car. I heard Ally scream from inside the vehicle as his hand wrapped around my throat and he lifted me, only to slam me back down again. It hurt, and it knocked the wind out of me for a moment, but I gathered my strength to slam into his arm with both hands like I was swinging an ax. It was enough to make him break his grip, and I shot my head forward to crash it into his face.

Blood spurted out from his mouth, and I kicked him in the gut, forcing him back a few steps. Still woozy, and upset by how much all this hurt more than usual, I stood on the roof of the car. I quickly measured him and the distance in my head and leapt. With one expert move, I twisted upside down, grabbed his head under the chin, and flipped down behind him, landing in a sitting position. I heard his neck snap as I landed and his body fell over me, all dead weight.

I stood and brushed off my pants as the two bloodied Fae stepped back. They seemed to value their necks. Naida woke up and was on her knees, watching as her backup ran away. Even the first Fae I'd knocked out cold was up and had taken off at some point in the skirmish. Fae were known for being fierce, but their will for fighting wasn't exactly legendary. Easy fights sure, but once the going got rough…

Naida spat blood at me. It landed on my shoe, and I smiled down at her.

"You think you're so—" she began, but I didn't let her finish. I rammed my knee into her jaw, and she went back down. As she struggled to her feet, I pulled out my switchblade.

No need to gather intel this time.

She saw the blade, and the fight left her. She leapt, her wings carrying her into the air. I pulled back my hand, ready to throw my knife and end this when her backup swooped toward me. I ducked, and when I looked back up, they were too far away.

I waved sarcastically after them as they flew off. "See you next time," I called. "Don't forget to write!" I slammed the car door as I got back in, then looked at Ally.

"How did they know we were coming this way?" she asked.

I thought for a second, then shrugged. "They're fucking fairies. Who knows how they do anything?"

I turned to look at Ally, but she hadn't moved. Instead, her hands were on the wheel, her head bowed. She was crying. "Hey, wait, what? What's going on?"

"This is never going to end, is it?" she asked through tears sliding down her cheeks.

"What, the Fae? Don't worry about it. I think I showed them that coming after us was a bad idea."

"They won't stop." She slammed her hands down on the steering wheel. I rarely saw her so upset, and my good mood vanished. "Don't you get it? You were so rough with them when you were getting intel that now they'll be looking for vengeance with you at every opportunity. There's nowhere you can go, nowhere you can hide. They will find you, and they *will* kill you, Slick. You embarrassed their leader, and they want revenge."

"Look, Ally," I began, trying to soothe her and defend myself at the same time. "The only way to deal with a Farsider is strength. When I was in The Deep, violence was all they knew, all they wanted, and all they did. They hate humans. No respect for us at all. Trust me. I am an expert on these things."

"They don't hate you because you're human. They hate you because you hurt them. And you hate them because they hurt you. Is that all the life that's left to you? Violence upon violence upon violence?"

"What do you expect me to do? Some problems require violence."

"It's not what you do that bothers me, it's who you're becoming," Ally accused. "You might be an expert on Farsiders, but I'm an expert on Sara Slick. I don't know all that happened to you in The Deep. I don't think I want to know. What I do know is terrible, awful things. Things I can't imagine living through. And I know it made you tougher, and maybe meaner, and it made you colder so you could do things to survive. But inside you is more than violence. Inside the heinous Sara Slick, there is still a girl who loves tacos and had a crush on emo boys from MySpace and loved her pink toe socks. Inside you is more than a fighter. Inside Sara Slick the warrior is Sara Slick, my friend. And that Sara is more than a weapon."

I sighed. Her words attacked that part of myself that Solon taught me to shut off. Maybe she was right. Perhaps I could have tried playing nicer with the Fae. But in my experience, Farsiders weren't stopped by a pretty smile. Until my family was safe, until Ally was safe, I'd be as heinous as I needed to be.

I looked at Ally but chose to keep my thoughts to myself. Even if I disagreed with her, it was still important to let her get it out. I had a head start when it came to Near/Far relations. And Ally had a right to get mad sometimes. After all, we had a decade of Best Friend Fights to make up for.

"When this is over, Ally, when all the fighting ends, I'll figure out how to be more than a weapon. I swear it."

"Yeah." Ally stuck her key in the ignition, wiped tears from her eyes, and started the car. "But with an attitude like yours, will that day ever come?"

CHAPTER ELEVEN

"Dam!" I shouted.

"What?" Ally shouted back, her voice reaching a death-defying pitch. "What? What's wrong? That spiky rat ball thing didn't throw up the cupcake cookie, did it?"

"No," I calmly replied.

"Then what the hell are you shouting about?" She clutched the steering wheel harder and snapped her eyes back and forth from me to the road.

"Dam." I pointed at the sign on the side of the road welcoming us to Hunt, West Virginia, and showing the direction of the town's water dam.

Ally rolled her eyes at me and continued down the road. Soon, we went around a bend, and the massive structure appeared in front of us.

"Dam!" I shouted again.

"What? What now?"

"Dam." I pointed at the huge structure. "Right there."

"What is wrong with you?"

"I'm being observant. Getting us familiar with our new surroundings." I swirled my hand around in the air in front of me to encompass the new town.

"Well, quit it."

The tiny town of Hunt nestled at the bottom of the dam, so it looked like it was almost sitting under it. A mining town from way back, it was the home of generations of people trickling down from the same families over the years. From the distance, the town was the definition of quaint as we drove toward it. Everything looked sleepy and quiet, old but not rundown.

"Did this Jonas guy mention to you he might be the only person who lives in this town?"

"There are more people who live here."

"Are you sure? Look at this place."

"I think it's adorable. So old-fashioned."

"I do, too. There have to be some happy little trees around here somewhere. Maybe a pond that didn't exist before there was light to reflect off it. A couple of puffy bushes. But what I don't see is people."

"Bob Ross never painted people. That's your problem right there. Can you get in touch with the Netherworld and see if his spirit can add a few for us?"

"It's not the Netherworld. It's The Far. We've been going over this for months now."

"Still working out the details, Slick."

"Damn," I muttered.

"I thought we said you weren't going to do that anymore."

"No, this time Splinter threw up his cupcake cookie."

At least he didn't eat all of it.

Hunt was even sleepier and more picturesque when we drove into it. Little shops and businesses looked like they'd been there since the town sprung up more than a century before to take advantage of mining the hills and mountains. There were no mega marts or bright, glaring trendy boutiques. No fast-food chains or clubs throbbing with music and flashing lights. No people.

It was still that last one throwing me off. After the Fae ambush, I was a little on edge and suspicious of everything around me. This place was so quiet. Like, we might have legit been painted into a scene, still and quiet. Which meant I was waiting for any second now when the entire place would split open and unfold into a monster with the cute buildings as legs like the Transformer from Hell.

Or The Far. There wasn't a lot of differentiation between the two at that juncture in my life.

"So, where are we supposed to stay?" I leaned forward to peer through the windshield at the darkness in front of us. A few lights twinkled in the windows of some buildings, and two streetlights glowed on either side of the street, but there were still deep shadows.

"Jonas made reservations for us at the hotel in town."

"Which hotel?"

"*The* hotel. Apparently, there's only one in town. It doesn't even have a name. Just 'Hotel.'"

"How ghost town of them."

It only took us a few minutes of driving to pull up in front of the large rectangular building with "Hotel" painted across the front.

"I think we found it," Ally commented.

We drove down a tight alley and around to the back of the building in search of a parking lot. Six dusty spots fulfilled that role. We climbed out slowly. When nothing disastrous happened within the first few seconds, I scooped Splinter up and stuffed him into my pocket. Each of us carried the big duffel bags we'd packed, and I brought an extra with a few weapons Archie sent along as we headed toward the door at the back of the building.

It creaked open, and a gust of cold air rushed out at us. That's one thing that never failed about hotels. It didn't matter where you were, when you were staying, or which hotel it was. The inside always had the thermostat set to Arctic Expedition. Except for mine. My hotel was a free spirit. It did what the wind told it to in terms of the inside ambiance.

We made it about five steps down the dark hallway before a shrill voice shouted at us. "That's the service entrance! Deliveries and outgoing mail only!"

Ally and I paused and looked at each other. We couldn't decide if the woman was serious or if this was some Hunt welcoming joke neither of us understood. When we didn't hear any laughter or encouragement to keep it coming, we decided she was probably serious and turned around. We hauled our luggage back out the door, through the parking lot, and up the alley around to the front of the hotel.

We walked through the front door, and the woman at the desk waved at us.

"That was a switch," Ally muttered under her breath at me.

"At least it's a human," I pointed out.

"Valid."

We walked up to the desk and the woman eyed us suspiciously. "Good evening."

"Hello," I said. "Lovely hotel you have here."

"Mmm-hmm," she responded. "Is there something I can do for you two? Do you need directions?"

"Directions? No." I shook my head. "We are in Hunt, right?"

"You are. That's the thing. We don't see too many outsiders around here."

That was at once comforting and extremely terrifying.

"We're here for a short time because we heard there might be something happening."

I raised one eyebrow at her while gauging her reaction. She didn't seem to care much, and nothing in her expression said she had any idea what I was talking about. If she was a Farsider wearing a little old lady-style people suit, she was fantastic at not giving it away. Ally sidled up beside me and gave the woman a sugary smile. The terse expression on the older woman's face immediately softened. That was Ally. She was always the sweet talker of the two of us. No matter what, she could talk her way out of—or into—almost any situation she wanted. That was why I never bothered to ask her what happened when she got home the night she smashed the Obama poster and I got arrested.

"Hi, there," she said. "We just arrived here in your beautiful little town. A friend of mine invited us to come and said he made a reservation here for us. Would you mind checking for me? It should be under Alejandra."

There they are. The forty-seven 'r's that I missed hearing roll out of her mouth when she said her name.

I checked back into the conversation from my misty-eyed reminiscing right around the time Ally cooed about the adorable barbershop she may or may not have pulled out of her ass because every tiny town has a barbershop. The woman, who I soon learned was named Edna, reached into the drawer in front of her and pulled out a room key.

"You're on the top floor. At the end, last room on your right. Oh, and I have this for you." She took out a note and handed it to Ally.

"It's from Jonas. 'Meet me at the bar.'" Ally flipped it over to look at the back, then flipped it over again and shook her head. "That's it."

I stared at the note, then looked at Edna. "Which bar?"

She gave me a withering look. "*The* bar."

"Thank you." Ally grabbed my arm and spun me around to head up the stairs before I could stick my tongue out at the woman. She knew me so well.

"*The* bar," I scoffed as we climbed the dark-carpeted steps to what Edna referred to as the top floor, but was the only floor other than the lobby. "She said that like I should instinctively know which bar she's talking about."

"We're in a town with one hotel and a stop sign, Slick. I don't think the nightlife is hopping around here."

"Well, at least she gave us a good room." I tried to be as optimistic as I could.

"She sent us to the absolute farthest room she could manage," Ally pointed out.

"Maybe it has a really good view."

"Let's drop off our stuff and go meet Jonas."

She unlocked the door, and we went into the room. It was everything I hoped for. The dark carpet and awkward florals only ever found in hotels made my heart soar. I loved hotels. I drew in a deep breath, smelled the cold, clean smell, and had to stop myself from tipping face-first onto the bed and staying there. It made me a little misty-eyed for my hotel room back home.

We dropped our bags onto the beds and unpacked them. I found a drawstring bag with a note taped to it in the bottom of mine.

"Looks like you got a present."

I opened it. "It's a note from Archie."

"What's it say?"

"Adds sparkle to any outfit. Directions for use: don't smash."

"How poetic."

"I guess it has something to do with this." I opened the drawstring bag and pulled out what looked like a large metal bracelet.

"He's giving you jewelry?"

I noted a hint of jealousy in her voice but didn't say anything about it. "I don't think that's what's going on here." I fished around in the bag with my fingers and came up with another note. "Actual directions for use: create a full moon and rotate toward your heart. It will protect you."

"Thank you for the clarity, Archie," Ally said.

I put the bracelet on and looked down at it. Carvings along the center depicted various phases of the moon. I noticed two half-moons on either side of the bracelet and touched them. They shifted under the touch, and I pulled them together. The inner part of the metal buckled and shifted like a puzzle until the two came together into the shape of a full moon. From there, I twisted it toward me. Nothing happened.

"Maybe it goes in the other direction."

I reversed the moon, and it unfolded itself, thick steel-like material falling into place so large that if I crouched behind it, I could fit my entire body. It was transforming into a shield. A damn good one too, by the look and weight of it, although I was thoroughly confused about how it fit inside the bracelet.

"Whoa." Ally stepped back from it. "He wasn't kidding."

"No. This thing is pretty serious. It won't give me any energy or strength, but at least it will stop some attacks against me."

"You're so cheerful. How do you make it go back?"

"I don't know." It took a few seconds before I managed to make the shield fold itself back down into the bracelet. "Like that. All right. Let's go find Jonas."

Before we could leave, a rustle in my pocket was followed by a large thump on the floor. I looked down to see Splinter weaving his way toward the bed. With considerable effort, he climbed up onto the comforter and looked back at me.

"Oh, all right," I muttered, then grabbed the pillows and arranged them together. Splinter happily crawled up into the middle of them and laid back while patting his tiny hand on his stomach.

"I take it he's not coming."

"Seems like he doesn't feel well. Maybe the cupcake got to him. He'll be fine here, just turn on the TV."

"For the rat?"

"For the rat."

Ally shrugged and hit the power button on the remote before tossing it down on the bed. The sounds of cartoons filled the room as Splinter burrowed himself a little deeper into the pillows and we walked out.

CHAPTER TWELVE

We decided to walk to the bar rather than folding ourselves back into the car for any longer. After the drawn-out drive, I looked forward to stretching my legs and letting my spine decompress.

As we wandered along the sidewalk, I caught movement out of the corner of my eye. Ally and I turned toward it at the same time and saw a tall figure walking down the middle of the street. I couldn't help being somewhat startled by him. I nudged Ally with my elbow.

"He's so tall," I whispered. "Like..." I gestured with my hands, pulling up with my fingertips from my palm and stretching them out to mimic his incredibly elongated figure.

"And young," Ally replied.

It hadn't occurred to me to look at his face since I was so busy being struck by the sheer amount of vertical space the man took up. When I looked closer, I saw how smooth and innocent his face looked. Not innocent in the way that came from not having seen the world or experienced any of it. I obviously didn't know anything about him, or what he had been through in the apparently very few years he'd been wandering around this earth. Instead, it was the type of innocence inherent in people as young as him. It was simply there, an accident of time.

But I'd learned that innocence didn't always coincide with what was beyond the face. That innocence lured people in, and that could make them all the more dangerous. Some of the eyes that still haunted my dreams stared back at me from faces as soft and innocent as this one. I instinctively moved closer to Ally as we passed him.

Considering it was the only one in town, the bar wasn't hard to find. It wasn't as eloquently named as the hotel they called Hotel. In fact, I didn't see a name on it at all. Instead, there was an open sign hanging over a door and the faint sound of music humming as we walked down the sidewalk toward it. I glanced back at the tall, young figure moving slowly down the street. There wasn't time to think about him any further. The music from the bar was louder as we got to the door and Ally opened it. We stepped inside and apparently found all the people in Hunt.

Or at least a good portion of them.

I was relieved to see this bar was almost nothing like the one I wandered into the first night I was out of The Deep. It was far smaller and had a far different vibe. Much like Linus's pumpkin patch, if there was such a thing as a bar being sincere, this was it. The bar itself was heavy wood and took up the majority of one half of the room. A row of black-cushioned stools snaked around it, close enough for the patrons sitting in them to chat if they wanted to, or wallow in their solitude if that was more their groove. The rest of the room featured a series of booths along the wall and a semi-circular stage tucked in one corner. An assortment of microphone stands told me there was going to be a band or some serious karaoke breaking out any minute.

I was hoping for the karaoke. I could belt out a mean "Summer Nights" if I found the right guy to be my Danny. I glanced around as Ally and I walked up to the bar and slipped onto two of the stools. No one jumped out at me as being T-Bird material. I might have to forego my musical expression for the evening. Or be seriously hardcore and go straight into ABBA.

A man beside me downed an entire pint of beer, followed it up with a handful of nuts, then washed that down with another pint of beer in about thirty seconds. Maybe this wasn't my audience.

"I don't think I've seen your faces around here." I looked in front of me and saw a kind-eyed woman with loose dark waves hanging below her shoulders and crinkles around her mouth that acted like a scrapbook of a life rich in both laughter and hardship. "You two visiting Hunt?"

Ally smiled at her. "Yes. We'll be here for the next few days."

"Good to hear. Always nice to meet new folks. At least some of us think so." Her eyes flickered to the end of the bar, where a man glared at us with the same suspicion Edna had. "But don't you let anyone bother you." She grinned and held out her hand to Ally. "I'm Shailene, the proprietor."

Ally shook her hand. "Ally. And this is Slick."

Shailene eyed me with a hint of a bemused smile on her

lips. I couldn't blame her. The woman had introduced me as Slick without any of those extra pesky letters that make up my first and the rest of my last name. She made me sound like I should be chewing a toothpick and performing petty crimes for Al Capone.

"It's nice to meet you," I said.

"You, too. What brings the two of you to Hunt?" Shailene asked.

"We're meeting a friend," Ally answered.

"Well, welcome. Can I get you something to eat?"

"Do you have tacos?" I asked.

Shailene shook her head. "Can't say we do. But we make a good burger. If you want, I can have them smash it up and sprinkle some chili seasoning on there for you." She stared at me for a few seconds, completely blank-faced, before she finally laughed. "I'm kidding. I wouldn't do that to an innocent burger. But we *really* don't have tacos."

"That was a roller coaster of emotions you put me through," I told her.

Shailene smiled. "So, a burger?"

"That would be great. Thanks."

She looked at Ally, who nodded. Shailene disappeared through the swinging door into the kitchen and I looked around. "Do you see Jonas?"

"No."

"Do we know what Jonas looks like?"

"I've seen a thumbnail of him."

"That's helpful." I sighed. "So, you're not Alejandr-rrrrrrrrrrrrrra today?"

She laughed. "Not today."

A form suddenly appeared on Ally's other side. The

massive, burly man squished himself onto the stool beside her and offered her what was probably supposed to be a dashing grin.

"Hi, there." He might have meant it as smooth and sultry, but it came out gruff and rumbling. "You must be new around here. I would have remembered a face like that."

"I'm visiting," Ally said.

"Then let me be the first to welcome you to Hunt."

"I've already been welcomed."

"Not by me. That's what really matters. I'm Cale."

"I'm Ally."

"I'm going to buy you a beer, Ally."

"Oh. No, thank you. I'm doing fine. High on life."

Awkward.

"Fine isn't good enough for someone like you, baby. I can make it so much better for you."

"I appreciate the offer, but I'm here hanging out with my bestie and waiting for a friend."

She was trying hard to be polite. I heard it in her voice. But I also saw the way she pulled away from him, her body tense. She was doing her best to brush him off, but Cale wouldn't take the hint. That was fine. I was a lot of things, but subtle wasn't one of them. I stood from my stool and was about to make sure the burly dude with the bad game took her hint. Before I could, another man stepped in.

He was young, with a chinstrap beard and sparkling eyes. Something about him said he was athletic, but not in the jock sort of way. The flannel shirt and backward base-ball cap gave off a sense of youth and contemporary atti-tude that didn't exactly fit in the town we were in, yet he moved and spoke as naturally as someone who had known these people for years.

"Hey, Cale, you're not making trouble for my guests, are you?" the man asked.

Cale grumbled something but slid off the end of the stool and walked away. "Come on. Shift at the mine is about to start," he said to a man hunched over in one of the booths.

Cale and most of the rest of the people at the bar walked away. When it quieted down, the man sat on the recently vacated stool. Shailene whisked out of the kitchen with our plates and scanned the suddenly almost-empty bar.

"There better be some cash left on those tables," she muttered as she set the burgers down in front of us. "How are you doing tonight, Jonas?"

Ally looked at him sharply, her mouth opening slightly when she saw his attractive face, and I leaned closer to her. "I thought you saw a thumbnail."

She nudged me with her elbow, and Jonas turned to smile at her. "Alejandra?"

"You can call me Ally."

"Ally, it's nice to meet you. I'm Jonas."

"It's nice to meet you, Jonas." Her voice slipped a little higher, and her eyes widened a little. If she batted her eyelashes any harder she might take flight.

"Why did you call her out here, Jonas?" I asked.

He chuckled. "Jumping straight to the point, aren't you?"

"Is there a reason I shouldn't?"

"Why don't you tell us a little about yourself?" Ally tried

to smooth out the somewhat rocky 'getting to know you' phase unfurling in front of me.

"Not too much to tell. I share Ally's fascination with the strange and unexplained. That's why I asked her to come here. I'm impressed by her work, and I knew she would be the ideal person to share this investigation. I trust her to understand it and help me get to the bottom of it."

"So, you don't work at the mine?" I asked.

"Oh, I'm not a coal miner. I'm not even from around here. I'm a civil engineer, in town for an assessment of the local dam."

He flashed a smile and gave Shailene a playful wink when she set a beer in front of him.

"Damn," I whispered.

Ally and Jonas both looked at me. Her eyes narrowed. "You're assessing the dam? That's... Why?"

I propped my elbow on the bar and rested my chin in my hand, staring at him as if fascinated by his job. It wasn't the most elegant of back-pedaling, but after I stuffed a few fries in my mouth without taking my eyes off him, he moved on.

"Hunt isn't all that different from other West Virginia mining towns. Old buildings. Generations of the same families. Traditions and roots that dig deep. I've been all over this state. I know what's normal. But there's something not normal here."

"Seems pretty normal to me." Ally sipped her beverage.

"On the surface, maybe. There's some sort of cult or commune that lives deep in the woods. They call themselves the Vrya." Jonas lifted his eyes to look at Shailene, who had moved over to the other side of the bar and was deep in conversation with an elderly man. He lowered his voice. "The townsfolk don't like to talk about the Freak-ahs. They're quiet and keep to themselves. They only come into town every once in a while to trade. When they do, they dress in strange clothing. It's like they don't know what clothes are appropriate for the climate or time. Sometimes they wear top hats with cowboy boots or sweaters and swimming trunks. It's weird."

Ally and I exchanged glances. This all sounded very familiar, and we were both thinking the same thing.

"Where do these people live?" I asked.

"That's the thing. No one knows for sure. I've spent a lot of time hiking and hunting around these woods, and I've never been able to find out where they are. As far as I can tell, no one has."

"If no one can find them, and they don't come into town bothering anybody, I'm surprised the townsfolk care," I said.

"I agree. It doesn't sound like much. And I didn't think too much of it until the murders started," Jonas continued.

"What murders?" Ally and I asked at the same time.

"It's been happening for a couple of weeks now. Three people have shown up dead in the mines. Their bodies looked really weird." Jonas drew a deep breath and looked around him conspiratorially. We leaned closer as he spoke barely above a whisper. "Like, they weren't normal. Freak-ishly tall, like they had been stretched. All cut up and scarred. I can only assume these people were tortured and mutilated. It's the only thing I can think of that would make them look so strange. The locals assume it's some weird cult ritual. Cops can't figure it out. I've tried to contact several papers and news organizations, but no one has shown up. I knew Ally would. I'm hoping she can shed some light on the situation."

"I'll try," she assured him.

His eyes suddenly moved to me and narrowed. "Who are you? What's your job?"

"I'm a photographer." The lie tumbled out of my mouth before I had a chance to think it all the way through.

Jonas's eyes brightened with excitement. "You are? That's fantastic. What kind of camera do you use? Sony A7 III? Canon EOS? Rebel SL2? Olympus Tough TG-5? That one's waterproof…"

"It's the point-and-shoot kind," I said.

He looked at me oddly, but before the conversation could continue, the ground rumbled beneath us, and I heard a loud boom.

"Oh, God!" Shailene cried. "It's a cave-in."

CHAPTER THIRTEEN

A plume of dust fell over the town like brown snow. It stung my eyes as I tried to run toward the source. Hunt was laid out fairly simply, with most everything branching off the cross-section of the two main streets.

The mine was a mile or so away, but since it was mountainous there, the road went straight up, and all the dust from the cave-in was settling onto the town. A large group of people joined us as we ran, everyone shouting and trying to help.

As we drew closer, a man stumbled by me, his clothes ripped and torn and his head a matted mess of dirt and blood. He seemed like he was in shock as he stumbled wildly away from the mine's entrance. I wanted to stop and help him, but at least he was out. More people would be trapped down there, and they needed to be my top priority.

Getting to the entrance required fighting through people running the other way. Some were helping others who were bleeding or were nursing visibly broken bones, and others were running for their lives. Panic set in, and those who handled it well started helping others. By the time we reached the entrance, there were a few others there helping people out.

Wave after wave of mostly able-bodied people came out, many of them coughing uncontrollably as the dust settled in their lungs. Some were covered in dirt to the point that only their wild and scared eyes blinked out at us. I tried to step into the entrance, but it was so dark I could barely see anything, so I stepped back out to find Ally. She was attending to a wounded person whose head nearly caved in despite his hard hat. He was babbling about something, and Ally was trying to soothe him.

Two ambulances roared down the street heading toward us, one from either side. That would help. They could take the wounded outside the mine to safety. The problem was the people still inside. I heard shouts and cries from deep within of people trapped, hurt, and panicking. I had to go back in.

I needed to help them. I knew it wasn't my town, and I was a stranger here, but there was an instinct in me to rush to where the trouble was. Something about my time in The Deep made me want to help as much as possible. I guessed it was better than if I had shut off and wanted to hurt everyone instead. Solon probably played a big part in that.

Three other men were running into the crumbling cave, and I took off with them. I heard rocks shifting, and the ground occasionally made a sound like the earth itself was trying to decide if it wanted to swallow everything and start over. There was but a short time to help these people out, and even then, we might be putting ourselves in more danger. Despite that fact, no one slowed down, least of all me, and we soon reached a pile of rubble where various voices came from inside, underneath, and behind.

We shoveled the rocks away in silence, tossing them to the sides of the cave so we didn't block our way in or out. More people filed in with us, ready to help carry survivors out. I threw rocks as fast as possible, trying to reach a body I saw through the debris.

I knew I was talking, I felt my vocal cords vibrating, but I couldn't process what I was saying. It was partly encouragement for them to stay with me, partly motivation for myself to remain calm and keep going, and partly anger at the fact that I was running out of time. Finally, I pulled the last large, jagged boulder off the hand and tossed it aside.

He was dead. The boulder I pulled off had crushed the back of his head, and his hand, which was now free, was only moving because of the cave's vibration. I was devastated, but I needed to keep moving. I pushed his arm out of the way and kept pulling rocks and tossing them aside. Thankfully, someone reached in and grabbed the body of the man I freed and hauled it away. If we had time, we would collect the dead.

If we had time.

The time seemed to go by so quickly, but as we kept working, the rubble cleared enough to make a pathway. The survivors came out one by one. We got them to safety outside, to the ambulances and doctors and nurses who hurried to the scene. Then we went back for the dead and dragged them out one by one until there seemed to be nothing left. I went back inside one last time and realized as I got halfway down the mineshaft that I was alone.

Everyone else was outside, secure in the thought they'd rescued everyone and were safe. But the mine was seconds from collapsing, and something tugged at me that I needed to go down again. I made it to the rubble and stepped past it, going through the pathway we created to let people out. It was a surreal feeling, going into danger so grave, so unyielding there was no way out, and for what? A feeling?

Then I heard a voice, meek and weak and desperate. It called to me from a few yards away in the cave's darkness. I stepped closer to it. I strained to see where I was since the darkness was overwhelming in its totality. I felt ahead of me while waiting for my eyes to adjust, and the voice came from below me.

"Help me," it said.

"I am, I'm trying. Are you trapped?"

"Yes." The 's' came out long and labored. I felt something ahead of me and reached for it. It was a large, heavy beam leveraged on top of him. My eyes slowly adjusted. I could barely make him out but could see that the beam barely missed impaling him. It was Cale, from the bar. He was trapped, scissored by the timber and the ground. I tried to lift it, but it wouldn't move. I needed more strength. I needed...

My locket.

Fuck.

Okay, something else. I needed to think of something else. Brute force wasn't going to work, and there was no time. I looked around us, trying to see in the almost pitch blackness.

"I'm trying, buddy. Hang in there," I heard myself say. He didn't respond. My thoughts went to the hand in the rubble from earlier, and I shook it off. There was no time for that. I needed to try, and then I had to get the hell out of there.

I came across a heavy steel bar while stumbling around. It was short and cylindrical, and my brain popped into engineering mode. If I could wedge it between the ground and the beam, maybe...

I shoved it into place beside the man, in between him and where the timber had the most room. If I could wedge it up a little more, I could pull him out. I tried pulling down to no avail. It was stuck really well, and I needed to create some space. I pushed and pulled, up and down, trying to wiggle it free. Frustration built up inside me, and finally, with a yell of anger, it moved. I pulled down as hard as I could. The timber lifted, only a few inches, but enough. The man groaned and rolled out of the way right as I lost my grip and the beam crashed down.

"Come on." I put his arm around my shoulder and hoisted him to his feet as best I could. "I got you."

We had crossed the rubble and headed up to the mouth of the cave when the rumbling began again, and the ceiling fell around us. I sped up our movements as much as possible, but a large chunk landed in front of us. A smaller piece fell just after and smacked the man in the back of the head, and his body became dead weight in my arms.

I had one trick left up my sleeve. I pulled the rune from my back pocket and activated the shield. It glowed white and yellow and crackled with energy, and formed a dome above me as I held it over my head like an umbrella. I reached down and grabbed the man by the waist. I didn't have time to think about how heavy he was, only that I needed to move him. I hoisted him up, draped his top half over my shoulder, and ran. The shield above me sizzled in the darkness and protected us from certain death.

Rubble and rocks and pieces of steel fell and bounced off the shield as I crested the top of the cave. We stumbled forward, my shield cutting off as we exited the cave and I fell to the ground. I spun to look into the cave one last time, and I swore I saw a figure. It stood unfazed, eyes glowing in the darkness. It was impossibly tall, and I realized that I recognized it. It was the man from the street right before we went into the bar.

Then he was gone.

I rubbed my eyes as the cave collapsed into itself. Voices swirled all around me, and the man I rescued was picked up by EMTs and whisked away. I did it. I rescued him. Safe in the knowledge of a job well done, I laid back in the dirt, exhausted, and closed my eyes for a second.

CHAPTER FOURTEEN

"Ow, that hurts. Ow, that hurts. Ow, that hurts. Seriously, I'm asking you to stop," I said.

The nurse put down what seemed like the fiftieth little alcohol-soaked gauze pad she had used to clean me up. She shot me a brief glare and picked up another one. "I have to get you clean. You don't want dirt from that mine all over you and getting ground down into these cuts."

"It really burns."

"It is alcohol."

"Well, my grandma always said alcohol was the work of the devil."

"I don't think this is the type of alcohol she was talking about, honey."

"It's also not anything my grandmother ever said. She drank tequila like it was going out of style."

"That's because Grandma Violet was *the shit*," Ally said from the doorway.

I looked at her, and she smiled as she came over to the side of the bed. They took most of the injured miners to the closest hospital, but I didn't want to go through that hassle. I insisted I was fine and didn't need to be seen by anybody. It was only a few scratches and scrapes, bumps and bruises. Your run-of-the-mill mine cave-in banged up situation. But Ally insisted I get looked at. So, she brought me to the local doctor's office.

"That she was," I agreed.

Ally looked at the nurse. "How is she doing?"

"She's a terrible patient," the nurse told her, but she said it through a little smile.

"Yep, that sounds like Slick. I'm surprised she let you get anywhere near her with that stuff. She'll use it on other people but freak the freak out if anyone comes at her with a bottle of alcohol."

"Care to tell her why?" I challenged.

"It wasn't that big a deal. I might have used a little too much when helping her clean up and gotten some in her ear," Ally told the nurse.

"And what were you doing right before that?" I prompted.

"Trying to pierce your belly button with a safety pin."

"If you were trying to clean her up after attempting to pierce her belly button with a safety pin, how did you end up getting rubbing alcohol in her ear?" the nurse asked.

"I think we're stumbling close to the reason I don't enjoy rubbing alcohol."

"Well, either way. What you did was amazing. Some people who were down in that mine literally owe you their life," Ally said.

"Just happy to help," I muttered. I waited for the nurse to walk out of the room and met Ally's eyes. "I saw something strange in that mine. As I was helping the last person out and we reached the edge of the cave, I looked back. Ally, that guy showed up."

"What guy?"

"The guy we saw walking down the street when we went to the bar. Remember? The really tall young one. He was down there. I have no idea where he came from, but he showed up and stood there while the mine caved in around him. Then he was gone."

"What do you think that means?" Ally asked.

I shook my head. "I'm not sure. It could be nothing."

Someone knocked on the door, and I called out, asking who it was.

"It's Jonas," he called back. "I wanted to make sure you're doing all right."

Ally looked at me for confirmation, and I nodded. She got up and hurried to the door to let him in. She gazed at him, obviously a little mesmerized by his good looks. He stepped into the room cautiously and walked up to the side of the bed.

"How are you feeling? Are you doing okay?"

"I'm fine. There was no reason for a doctor to see me. I'm a little bounced around, is all. But Ally insisted I see someone and have them help me clean up all these extensive injuries you see in front of you."

"Ally sounds like she's an excellent friend," Jonas said.

Ally tossed a smug, self-satisfied look in my direction. "I told you."

"She wiped me off with a bunch of alcohol pads. You could have brought me home and spritzed me with Windex, and it would have had the same effect."

"I always loved being appreciated for my professional work," the nurse said as she came back into the room carrying a handful of bandages.

I cringed. "I'm sorry. That didn't come out right. It's only that I've been through a lot, and had to learn to deal without doctors."

"Is this another incident involving her and safety pins?"

"No. This one's not her fault. I appreciate your help. Now that my skin doesn't feel like it's melting off, I feel better."

"I'm glad to hear it." She wrapped up the worst of my scrapes and scratches with bandages and left the room again.

"I'm impressed by you, you know," Jonas said. "What you did back there was incredible."

I tried to brush it off by looking away and sweeping my hand around in the air in front of him to dissipate the words. "It's not that big a deal. Anyone would have done it."

"That's the thing. Nobody did," Jonas answered me. "How many people stood around outside the mine, waiting?"

"Hey," Ally snapped. "Not all of us are equipped with the fortitude and skills to manage the disaster relief efforts of a mine cave-in."

"And that's perfectly fine. That's what makes what she did so impressive."

"I told her that, too," Ally agreed.

"Can we get back to talking about why we came here?" I wanted to steer the conversation away from me.

"Are earthquakes normal around here?" Ally asked.

It was kind of a jump, but I would take it. Jonas shook his head.

"Again, I'm not from around here, but I've visited this area many times. Earthquakes didn't used to happen around here. But now...now it's different. It's starting to feel like a pattern. Every time a body turns up, an earthquake happens soon after."

"That's a pretty big warning sign," Ally pointed out.

"This was the first time there was a cave-in. The earthquakes are getting worse."

I swallowed hard when the realization of what that meant sank in. I drew a deep breath and readied myself.

"So, that means—" I started, but he mercifully stepped in to stop me from having to ask the question directly.

"Yes. They found another body. It's right down the hall if you want to see it."

CHAPTER FIFTEEN

We crept down the hallway toward the room that was doubling as a morgue after the cave-in but stopped short when we saw a doctor lingering right outside. We backed up into a dark alcove lined with racks of newly cleaned lab coats.

"We have to get around that doctor," Jonas said. "I don't think he would like us wandering in for a meet and greet with their newest corpse."

I looked at the coats hanging from the metal rack. "We could put these on. Pretend that we're doctors, too, and need to check on the bodies."

Two sets of eyes in full judgment mode turned on me.

"Then maybe we can do a montage of investigating the body to the smooth sounds of Wham! before doing a slow-motion run out of the office and back to the hotel with everyone on our heels." Ally didn't hide her sarcasm.

"Well, that sounds like a delightful movie. Do you have another suggestion?"

"I could talk to him, pretend I need his help with

someone outside, then run like hell and meet you when you leave," she offered.

"That's a better plan. Do your thing."

"Are you sure about this?" Jonas asked. "We don't want to make them suspicious."

"Trust me. She won't. I mean, at some point she will, but that's kind of built into the plan with the whole run like hell part. It's a process."

He didn't look entirely convinced, which was understandable. Ally shook out her hair and smoothed her clothes, then slapped on a compelling concerned face and burst out of the alcove toward the doctor. Jonas and I sank backward into the hanging coats so we wouldn't be seen when other staff heard the commotion and came down the hall to see what was happening.

"See? I knew these coats were going to come in handy for the plan," I whispered.

Jonas rolled his eyes at me and peered around the corner at Ally. My best friend chattered and gasped while rambling to the doctor about needing help and asking him to come with her. I couldn't understand the majority of the words coming out of her mouth, but I was sure that was the intention. If she could confuse the doctor badly enough, her big eyes and pouty lips would be enough to get the man to come along. It took less than thirty seconds.

Ally ran down the hall in the opposite direction with the doctor following close behind her. Jonas and I waited for a few seconds before stepping out of the alcove and hurrying over to the door.

"What's she going to do when she gets that guy outside, and nobody is waiting?" Jonas asked.

"Didn't you hear the plan?" I grabbed the handle and tugged on it despite the obvious keypad keeping it secure. For such a small town, I was shocked to see them have anything more complicated than a mass-produced key lock, but I guessed they treated the rare dead-and-not-at-the-hospital with a little extra care.

"The plan is for her to go out there, not have anyone injured or gravely ill, or having been abducted and probed or whatever the hell she was rambling about, then run?"

I swung my eyes toward him. "Do you have some brilliant other plans you decided to keep tucked in your back pocket for the next time we need to break into a morgue?"

"No," he admitted.

"Then we'll let her handle it." I ran my fingers over the keypad while trying to figure out how to overcome it.

"Is there an emergency button that overrides the need for a code?" Jonas asked.

"That seems like it might be a bit of a design flaw, don't you think?"

"I don't think she'll be able to keep up the charade for very long. We need to figure out how to get in there."

There was only one option. Two, if someone happened by with a friendly disposition and willingness to put the code in for us. That left me with relying on one. I reached into my pocket and pulled out my switchblade. "I'm going to ask you to take a step back. I've never done this particular procedure before, and I'm not sure exactly what's going to happen."

"What is that?"

"A switchblade."

I examined the edge of the keypad until I found where

it connected, and used the tip of the blade to pop the plastic cover out of place. It revealed a series of wires, and I took a few seconds while thinking about which one of them would be most effective to cut. Deciding it wasn't a bomb, so the chances weren't great it would explode, I picked them all up in one hand and used the blade to slice through them cleanly. There was no massive flash of light or big boom, so I took it as a victory.

The door opened when I turned the handle and pushed. Jonas and I slipped inside, and I closed the door behind us.

"Who are you?" he asked again, more suspicious this time after watching me disable the keypad.

"I told you. I'm a photographer. With my Sunny 85-15 AAA Gumball." I tucked my trusty switchblade away.

"I thought you said you had a point-and-shoot."

I narrowed my eyes at him. "That *is* a point-and-shoot." I was going to ride this thing as far as it would carry me.

"The body is over here." He directed me to the nearest drawer.

We pulled it out, and my hand flew to my mouth. There wasn't enough time between learning about the body from the mine and me getting here to develop any expectations about it. Even if there had been, I didn't think it would be anything like this. This wasn't merely any body. This was the body of a Farsider.

"I can't believe this," I murmured.

"I told you someone put him through something pretty horrible." Jonas pointed out a few areas of the body. "This looks like ritualistic mutilation. I wouldn't be surprised if it were part of some sort of ceremony."

I understood why he would say that. Anyone looking at

the poor man stretched out on the table would see the strange areas of the body and think they were mutilations. I knew different. I'd seen this before. What Jonas called mutilations were dryad attributes. I had encountered those creatures during my time in The Deep and knew how to recognize the unique features.

Long arms and legs stretched down until they almost fell off the slab entirely. The skin, if that's what you would call it, was hard and thick, and seemed to grow separately in batches that then wove together in layers. It looked for all the world like tree bark. Nearsider legends spoke of dryads as 'tree spirits,' and there was no doubt why that was so. The big, sunken eyes of this one seemed friendly, if rather Neanderthal-ish. Its fingernails were brown and chipped in jagged lines like they had grown for a long time, but had broken near death. His empty, lifeless eyes looked up at the ceiling in the thousand-yard stare of the dead I had seen so many times before.

But it wasn't only those attributes that struck me about the horrific corpse of the slightly older man spread out on the table. This man had also been severely beaten. It was savage, brutal in its extent. Wounds covered every part of the body, leaving it tattered. Whoever did this hated this person. I drew in a breath, then slowly let it out. It was a horrible sight, and I had seen my fair share of horrible. This would have been a terrorizing experience that could have taken a long time to finally result in death.

I couldn't tell much about him. The injuries were too extreme to be able to identify many details. Even if I knew who he was, it might have been a challenge to recognize him immediately. This needed more evaluation. I took out the phone Ally got for me and started snapping pictures of the body while walking around the perimeter of the slab to get images of him from all angles.

"Why aren't you using your camera to do that?"

Still trying to get me. *I'm one step ahead of you, buddy.*

"You can't possibly think I'd have my Gumball with me here. That is a delicate, high-dollar piece of equipment. I don't traipse it out wherever I might need to snap a picture or two."

"We should get out of here."

"Yeah, we should probably find Ally." I stuffed my phone back into my pocket.

I stuck my head out of the morgue and looked up and down the hallway to make sure no one was there. It was still empty, so we slipped out and headed for the door leading outside.

A few doctors had gathered around and talked heatedly.

"She left. I didn't get the chance to look her over or give her discharge papers," one said.

"Oh, shit. They're talking about me. Go. Go, go, go."

We scurried around the edge of the parking lot and rushed out onto the main road. I reached for my phone to call Ally, but she jumped out from behind a tree at me. My hand smashed against my heart, and I shook my head at her.

"You are so lucky I didn't have my switchblade in my hand right then. Come on. We need to get away from here. They're looking for me. Probably you, too."

Ally looked at Jonas. "Thank you. I appreciate you getting in touch with me and helping us."

Jonas nodded. "No problem. Call me anytime, okay?" He pointed to a red SUV on the side of the road. "But for right now, I've gotta run. I'll call you soon."

With a little wave, Jonas got in his car, and we parted ways. Ally and I walked back to the hotel, and when we got into our room, I latched the door and took out my phone. "Look at this. I took pictures of the body."

"Holy hell, what happened to him? Is it a Farsider?" she asked when she looked at the screen and scrolled through the pictures.

"Without a doubt. And someone wanted him to suffer. I think it's time we found this commune."

CHAPTER SIXTEEN

Splinter squirmed as I tried to get him safely to the ground, and when his little feet hit the dirt, he took off in circles, delighted to be out of my pocket and in nature, and obviously feeling much better after the horror that was 'The Cupcake Incident.'

"I thought Splinter was more of a city kind of guy." Leaves crunched under Ally's feet as she walked.

"Splinter is an 'anywhere food might be left out' kind of guy, but yeah, he seems pretty stoked about the woods."

Ally laughed in an easy way that was good to hear. She hadn't been very relaxed since the last Fae attack, and I thought getting some fresh air would be good for her nerves. I wanted to keep the mission talk to a minimum so I could give her a break, but Ally brought it up anyway, although she didn't seem as down today.

"So, what did Archie say?"

Earlier, I called Archie to talk about what I saw at the doctor's office and to thank him for the shield. I also emailed him the pictures I took, which resulted in a much longer conversation than I hoped for.

"Well, he was happy the shield worked out well. I told him how it held up in the cave and how it saved my life and that guy. He was pretty pleased with himself over that."

"Sounds about right." Ally used a large stick she found earlier to be her walking stick to stab the ground as we went up a hill.

"Then I sent him pictures of the body from the morgue. Definitely a dryad. There are a bunch of different varieties, and he isn't sure which one, but some of them are pretty dangerous. He also said they're known to cause earthquakes occasionally, so, you know…"

"So, be careful."

"Yeah."

"Yeah."

"Anyway," I tried to liven up the situation and make it less about the constant fear of death and dismemberment, "I thought if you wanted to, we should come up here and camp sometime."

Ally stopped dead in her tracks, and I awaited her response. It could go either way into righteous indignation that I would try to cheer her up with a camping trip, or a happy squealing sound capable of waking up the gods themselves and starting an avalanche a thousand miles away. I squinted and waited for either one.

Somewhere, an avalanche mysteriously fell, and thousands of dogs lost their ever-loving minds for a minute.

When she finished squealing and shaking me by the shoulders while jumping up and down like she won the Showcase Showdown on *The Price is Right*, I smiled back at her and tried to focus on the vibrating girl in front of me.

"So, that's a yes?"

"Eeee!"

"All right, then. I'm glad you're excited. Hell, I'm excited."

What shocked me was, I wasn't lying. The prospect of camping excited me. It was a novel thing for me, something I would never have imagined myself feeling, but I was trying it out. It had been a couple of months since my escape from The Deep, but that handful of weeks compared to the decade of captivity in the slimy walls of the prison left me craving the air and sunshine. I would happily roll around in the grass and pine needles simply because I could. I didn't need to do anything to convince my best friend. Ally was already all in.

"God, how many times did I try to talk you into camping with my family?" Her voice was still several octaves higher than it should be.

"At least three."

"Try a hundred. Maybe a thousand. Oh, man, Slick, this will be so much fun. We'll bring a telescope and some marshmallows and chocolate and graham crackers, and..." she started rattling off.

"Bug spray and a lighter," I interrupted. Ally looked at me with her jaw agape, as if I had besmirched her entire family.

"Bug spray, yes, obviously, but we don't need a lighter. We can use flint to start a flame. I learned all about starting fires. I have badges and everything," she said snootily. But I saw the grin behind the snoot.

"Yes, yes, you're the survivalist girl, I'm only a girl who lived in a murderous prison for a decade. You totally have me on the 'don't die' skills. Seriously, though, I think that after all that time in a dark, dank location, a night under the stars sounds fun. Especially hanging out with you," I quipped.

"Aww, thanks, bestie." She nudged me with her hip. "So, fresh air and sunshine aren't your mortal enemies anymore?"

"We'll see." I laughed. We crested a hill and were in a large outcrop of trees that led back down into a gorge ahead. In the distance, there was a clearing that overlooked the area, and I started us toward it. It seemed like the perfect place to stake out a camping spot.

As we neared the area, Ally ran out into the middle of the open space and twirled around, a smile breaking across her face. She was already planning the menu and order of operations for our night camping when I noticed something was wrong. It was Splinter. He stood stock-still several feet in front of me, up on his hind legs, but not like he was begging or looking for something to eat. This was an aggressive stance. A low growl came from deep in his belly.

I turned to see what he was looking at, but the tree line looked empty. The area we stood in was also empty, and there was a gorge on one side. Whatever he sensed, I couldn't see it, but years of trusting his instincts taught me to be alert. I touched the shield rune disguised as a bracelet on my arm and reached in my pocket for the switchblade. Ally, dizzy from spinning, stopped to look at me. Her face screwed up in the way it did when she smelled something particularly rank. Then her eyes went wide, and her jaw trembled. A hand rose, and she pointed behind me. Splinter shrieked, and I spun in time to dodge a sharpened stick thrown at my back.

It was a dryad, maybe seven feet tall, and he was running toward me. Unlike the dry, gray dead thing with the kind-looking eyes, this one was green and brown and brimming with life in his eyes. He was also determined to end a life, notably mine. With no time to think, I rolled to my right. It took the dryad off-guard, and he stumbled to a stop and turned toward me. As he did, Splinter jumped up and bit him on the ankle. It seemed to have little to no effect, and I activated the shield.

The dryad punched me, but the shield blocked the blow. His hand crunched into the protective magic, and he cried out in pain. Using the shield like a weapon, I swung the energy field up until it crashed into his jaw and sent him onto his back. After flicking the switchblade open, I prepared to move in for the kill when Ally screamed.

I looked up to see the clearing swarming with dryads. Some of them were more tree-like than their companion, and they wore various levels of clothing. While the one on the ground only had shorts on, some of these had t-shirts and long pants. One or two even wore shoes. There had to be ten or more of them, and some were circling Ally. I ran to her, jump-kicking one as I drew near. Without the locket, I couldn't get as high on my jumps as I was used to and lamely kicked him in the chest.

It wasn't what I'd seen in my mind, but it was enough to knock him back into a smaller dryad, and they both crashed to the ground. Another reached for me, but I sliced his arm with the switchblade. He cried out and another took his place. I kicked it low but felt like I did more damage to my leg than to him. Switching up my tactic to one that had worked before, I slammed the shield into his chest and sent him sputtering backward.

"Ally, run," I screamed while trying to fend off the dryads circling us. If I could get her safe, she could get in touch with Archie, maybe find help. Unless the trees killed me. In that case, they would at least know to run and never look back.

Ally took off the way we came, and a huge dryad stepped in front of her. He blocked her movement and reached out to grab her. In my panic, I threw the switchblade at him, and it landed in his shoulder. He roared in pain and fell to his knees. The rest of them closed in on me now, and I ran to the one I stabbed. Ally was now yards away, and I yanked the blade out of his arm. As I did, I turned to follow Ally and met a tree trunk arm that punched me so hard I flew backward into the wooded area. I hit the ground hard, and my vision dimmed. I tasted blood in my mouth, and my body refused to respond.

The last thing I saw was Ally, kicking and screaming while being taken away under the arm of the dryad I had stabbed with my switchblade. My mouth opened to protest, but no sound came, and slowly, my eyes shut.

CHAPTER SEVENTEEN

Nothing wakes you up quite like sharp little Splinter feet in your face. Usually, I hated it when my animated toilet brush-looking pet decided to do an early morning dance on my forehead to inform me I should be up and giving him something to eat.

He didn't do it often because he was lazy, but when he did, oh, he really got into it. But considering it wasn't morning and Splinter had already eaten plenty, his efforts to wake me up didn't bother me nearly as much. I crushed my eyes closed more tightly for a few seconds, silently evaluating my body to make sure nothing was broken or missing.

The next stage was gradually feeling my arms and legs to make sure they were there and intact. I'd like to think I was the type of person who would be able to tell if a large chunk of me was removed while I was asleep, but you can never be too sure.

I was finally confident I was not only alive but still in as much of one piece as when I walked into the woods. I opened my eyes and looked around. It looked like I was still in the same place I was when fighting the dryads. My head rang as I pieced together my memory of the fight, but what I remembered most clearly was watching Ally get dragged away.

I had no idea how much time passed between seeing that and waking up. The light around me was different, and the change indicated I had been out for a while. At least an hour, maybe more. That meant she could be anywhere by now.

Trying to scramble to my feet proved unpleasant at best and jarringly painful at worst. The fight with the dryads left me sore, but not seriously harmed. I couldn't feel any blood running down my skin, and my muscles were all ready and willing to get me moving. It was the pain that made jumping to my feet not exactly the best option for the moment. Instead, I rolled over onto my hands and knees. I wasn't exactly standing yet, but I was no longer sprawled out on the forest floor. I would accept that as a victory.

Splinter scurried over to me and rubbed his prickly side against my face. He made a chattering sound I recognized as happiness and once thought was a potential precursor to him completely snapping and taking us all out. I wouldn't put it past Splinter. I still found him absolutely adorable and loved him dearly, but it didn't escape me that I still had no clue what he was, and therefore didn't really have a frame of reference for how he might behave in different circumstances. It was all about learning as we went between Splinter and me.

"Have you seen Ally? Did you see where they took her?"

Splinter stared back at me without saying a word. He was kind of the strong, silent type that way. It wasn't particularly helpful at the moment. I got to my feet and looked around. There was no sign of Ally or the dryads I had seen holding her. When I first woke up, there was a moment of hope. I thought maybe the blow to my head mixed up all the signals in my brain and I didn't see my best friend getting abducted by bark-covered Farsiders. Perhaps the fight was too intense, and they moved her out of the way because she didn't pose a threat to them. She could be curled up somewhere nearby, waiting for me to find her.

But then, why leave us? Where were the dryads, and what was the point of the fight?

That wasn't what happened. She wasn't around here anymore for the same reason the dryads weren't. They took her.

My lungs protested as I tried to pull in as much air as possible and hold it. When it wouldn't stay in there any longer, I forced myself to release it in a long, controlled stream. I repeated the action, willing myself to absorb all the anxiety and fear from throughout my body and push it out in the breath. It sounded like one of the completely whacked out things my hippified PE teacher in middle school would have said. I thought it was bunk then, and I still thought it was bunk, but I'd be willing to string myself in crystals and perform a stylized swimming event in a pool of essential oils if I thought it might keep me calm.

I was doing everything I could not to panic. Of course, a surefire way to create panic is to try to convince yourself and others there was no reason to panic. Which was what spiraled my mind out of control. It cycled through a brutal slideshow of my time in The Deep.

Every moment that flashed in front of my eyes was another of the terrible things the Farsiders threatened to do to me during my ten years there. And then some of the things they actually did to me. They might not be serving sentences in The Deep, but I knew other Farsiders were more than capable of fulfilling those threats and various other creative options I hadn't even heard of.

Which meant I needed to snap the hell out of my thoughts and find my best friend before she got ground up by the hoof of a centaur and stuffed into a goblin's intestine to be used as breakfast sausage. That one was courtesy of a particularly delightful troll angry with me for standing in the patch of imaginary sunlight coming through his imaginary window.

I looked around frantically and noticed a small trail leading away from where I woke up. Was that where they went? I couldn't remember if that was the direction they were going when I saw them snatch Ally. Disoriented and confused after hitting my head on whatever I landed on, I could barely process what I saw, much less retain where she was. But a path seemed like the best option. If I couldn't find anything in that direction, at least I'd be able to make my way back and try again.

Splinter ran for all he was worth at my feet as I took off down the path. I ran until it seemed I had gone far enough without seeing any signs of them. Not wanting to waste time, I turned back and started again. I paid close attention to my surroundings. Every time I walked deeper into the woods, I looked around for any sign that Ally might have come this way.

When we were in high school, there was a string of murders in a nearby college town. All the victims were girls in their late teens. It was short-lived and fortunately didn't get any more extreme than three bodies, but it was enough to inspire the motivational speaking cogs of every principal within a thousand-mile radius to go into overdrive.

We thought most of it was ridiculous, of course, because we were teenagers and teenagers know everything. It's a proven fact. Ask the internet.

But one thing we took seriously was the recommendation to have a plan in case we found ourselves in a dangerous situation. They told us to get in the habit of telling people when we were going to leave home, where we would be, and approximately how long we would be gone. That seemed all well and good to us, but somewhat on the too little, too late side for me. After all, by the time someone noticed you weren't back when you were supposed to be, any number of horrific things could have happened. Instead, Ally and I committed ourselves to come up with ways to keep ourselves safe, rather than ways to direct people to find our bodies.

In the end, we still planned for the search-and-rescue portion. After agreeing no one would take us out without putting up a hell of a fight, we promised each other if someone ever tried to abduct us, we would leave as much evidence as possible. That meant touching every single surface we could get our hands on, leaving hair in the person's car, and creating a trail for whoever was out looking. But there was nothing around here. No pieces of her clothing, no chunks of her hair. She didn't leave behind any bits of herself, which meant one of two things. Either this wasn't the way she had come, or they incapacitated her to the point of not being able to leave the clues. Neither seemed like a fantastic option. I didn't want to think about her vulnerability.

After several hours, I was still clawing my way through the woods. Experience held me back from screaming for her immediately. It wasn't subtle enough and could put her in more danger depending on who had her and for what reason. Finally, I had to come to terms with reality. I was looking for any clue at all, but there were none. I needed help.

CHAPTER EIGHTEEN

I was exhausted. Every part of my body protested against me trying to run. The muscles in my legs burned and ached. My joints felt stiff and didn't want to move. Even breathing felt like a struggle as I pushed myself to keep going. But it didn't matter. I wouldn't stop. Wherever the dryads had taken Ally, she was in danger. I couldn't ignore it or pretend she would be fine. I couldn't tell myself it was all right to slow down and listen to my body trying to drag me back onto the ground because someone else would be there to protect her. I learned many things during my years in The Deep, but one of the most valuable was never to believe someone else would be there to do what needed doing. I had to do it myself.

Even Solon. My trusted friend, my mentor, the one who kept me alive and ensured I knew how to keep myself alive. I could never drop my guard and rely on him showing up or saving me. He taught me that himself. He wanted me to know and understand it from the very beginning. All life is fleeting. Life in The Deep is a continuous gauntlet. Solon didn't know from moment to moment if he would be able to come back and help me, so he taught me it was my responsibility to trust when I could, but never overlook my commitment to myself.

That meant it was up to me to save Ally. Lying unconscious on the soggy ground of the forest was a speed bump in the process. If I'd sustained the head blow without going unconscious, or was able to wake up within a few minutes, it would have been much easier to track her down. But much longer than that had passed, and they had disappeared.

There was no telling how far they'd gotten by now. Dryads could move. Their tremendous height helped them cover more ground, and their strength meant if they wanted to, they could toss Ally along through the forest like an Ally bucket brigade.

I couldn't trust anyone else to step in and figure it out for me, but I did need some help. Ally was tough and was getting stronger every day, but she wasn't a fighter and didn't have anywhere near the necessary experience to help her handle a battle like this against Farsiders. Dryads were extremely tough, and not knowing exactly what they wanted with her made it more frightening. I needed someone with insight into the area and the situation unfolding around us.

That meant I needed to find Jonas. Jonas told Ally that he wasn't from the area, but he was there for an extended work project. He maintained a house near the central part of town so he didn't have to spend his entire life in the hotel, despite its charms. In any of the other places I'd been since leaving The Deep, having only the vague concept that a person lived in the area and knowing I needed to find them would be a daunting, seemingly impossible prospect.

Not so much with Hunt.

One distinct benefit of existing inside a Bob Ross painting of rustic West Virginia was there weren't a lot of options when it came to finding a house. I had a vague idea of where he lived and knew what his car looked like. It was enough for me to go on. But I made a quick mental note to always ask for the exact address of anyone I might need. Possibly GPS coordinates as well.

My exhaustion didn't hold me back as I made my way back through the forest and into town. I made good time getting back into the main part of Hunt and the tiny neighborhood on the outskirts. Now it was only a matter of narrowing down the options and finding which house belonged to Jonas.

It made me wonder about him as I made my way up and down the streets. He obviously cared about this area and knew a lot about what was happening. But I wondered how long it had taken him to get in touch with Ally. The body lying in the morgue hadn't been dead for long. Maybe if he had acted faster and figured out something sooner, that man wouldn't be dead.

On the other hand, what was he supposed to do? He said he contacted many other people, and no one would take him seriously. There was a little bit of the being chosen last for the game of dodgeball in elementary school gym class feeling to being the last resort, but at least he reached out to her. It was fortunate he did. Any of the others would have been looking for a cult and trying to figure them out. I knew what we were really dealing with. I merely had to figure out what to do to stop them.

I finally spotted Jonas's SUV sitting in the driveway beside a slumbering little ranch in a row of houses that looked almost exactly the same. It had the effect of Christmas cookies lined up for decoration. They all had the same basic shape and some of the same features, but the details varied slightly from home to home.

Some had flowers in the boxes in front, and some had flags hanging by the door. One had a bright pink mailbox festooned with a vibrant glass and metal sculpture of a flamingo, and I wanted to be friends with whoever lived there.

Jonas's house was quiet and plain. No flowers. No flag. Definitely no flamingo. The house sat a few yards back from the edge of the road on a square of grass fading from the season. I looked at the car more closely as I approached to make sure it was the right one. I recognized it as the one he got into at the doctor's office, right down to a sticker in the bottom corner of the back window. This was his house, and he was there.

At least, that was my theory. It got shakier when I walked up the sidewalk onto the front porch and realized the front door was standing ajar. The interior I could see through the gap in the door was dark. Not a single light illuminated any of the rooms.

"Jonas?" I called in through the gap. "Jonas, are you there?" There was no response, and I leaned in further, sticking my mouth into the gap of the door. "Jonas? I need to talk to you. It's about Ally."

When there was still no response, I used my foot on the

bottom of the door to ease it the rest of the way open and slipped inside. The first room of the house was a small living room. A couch, coffee table, and TV sitting on a stand were all that took up space. That was all I got to see. The rest of the house was incredibly dark, but I didn't want to turn on a light and alert anyone outside that I had snuck in.

Or leave fingerprints. But that was a thought I didn't want to dwell on at the moment.

I relied on my instincts and what I could sense around me as I moved further into the house, calling Jonas's name as I went. I turned down a hallway and heard rustling behind me. My breath caught in my throat as the hinges of a door creaked slightly. It could have been the wind coming through the front door and moving another one.

It also could have been a big drooling guy waiting for me around one of the invisible corners. *Damn it, Ally.* Why did she have to talk about the woodboogers? Of all the lovely wildlife living its life in West Virginia, she had to go straight to the foul-smelling, forest- and swamp-dwelling cousin to Bigfoot. Just what I needed.

I could have turned and run, but I was Sara Slick. That shit wouldn't fly.

I kept going. My breath sounded loud as I made my way farther down the hallway while struggling to get my eyes to adjust to the darkness inside. I took another step, and the creaking hinges sounded again, this time right behind my head.

I whipped around to face the sound, and a dark figure bounded out of the room at me. It reached out to wrap its hands around my throat as I screamed and dove away.

My body smashed to the ground. I tried to scramble away, but a hand clamped onto my ankle and yanked me backward. A strong grip pulled me up off the floor.

"What are you doing here?"

I immediately recognized the voice.

"Holy shit, Jonas. What is wrong with you? I thought you were a woodbooger."

He set me on my feet. "Well, that's a colloquial one. I don't think they frequently wander into houses."

"And I didn't think people usually hung out in the pitch dark not answering when someone calls for them a million times. Yet, here we are. Can we turn a light on or something?"

He guided me back into the living room and turned on a lamp. "I'm sorry. I had my headphones on. I must not have heard you. What's going on?"

"It's Ally. I need your help."

CHAPTER NINETEEN

"…and that's when we were attacked," I said.

"By who?" A mixture of fear and excitement laced Jonas's voice. I didn't want to tell him everything and was planning on explicitly not telling him the attackers were Farsiders. That would get into a whole other thing, and I didn't have time for all that right now. But his eyes were full of questions, and he was particularly suspicious of me since he met me, and I wondered how long I could keep up the charade.

Hopefully, long enough to find Ally.

"I don't know. I didn't get a very good look at them, but there were a bunch of them, and they moved very fast. They knocked me out before I knew what was going on and when I woke up Ally was missing," I half lied. Technically, all the elements of truth were there. They happened to be peppered by a couple of misleading words and one outright lie.

"We need to call the police," he said firmly.

Fuck.

"No, we can't." Jonas stared at me like I had three heads for a second, then shook his head and blinked a few times, apparently trying to process why a woman who was attacked and her friend kidnapped didn't want to call the cops.

"That has to be the most ridiculous thing you've said to me since we met, and you've said some ridiculous bullshit up to now." He pulled out his phone.

"You haven't heard the half of it," I muttered. "Seriously, we can't call the cops. It won't help. There has to be a better way."

"Than the cops? The people who investigate crime? Like assault and kidnapping?" His voice rose with each question. Then he sat heavily in his chair. A noise came out of him that sounded like a cross between exasperation and laughter, and he looked into my eyes before speaking again. "Who the hell are you? I know you aren't a photographer. A Gumball? Really? Who are you? For real. No bullshit."

"No bullshit?" He had no idea what he was asking. If I gave up the ghost on this character I was playing for him, it meant blowing the whole shebang open. It was a massive violation of the *Pax Philosophia* and could lead to him losing his shit and either calling the cops on me or assuming I was insane and kicking me out.

"I would like a very minimal amount of bullshit, please." He crossed his arms in front of him, and I sighed heavily. Well, it's not like they could do anything to me. What would they do, extend my life sentence?

"All right. The truth. Do you know what Fae are?" I began.

It took about twenty minutes of me talking, shushing him when he had questions, and allowing me to barrel through it. I explained the concept of The Near and The Far, and how I came from one to the other and back again, although I left out the whole 'convicted of heinous crimes and a felon on the run' stuff. For some reason, I felt like it wouldn't exactly help my case. When I got to the part about the Vrya who attacked me, and how I needed to get to wherever they were hiding rather than call the cops and bring them into it, he was shaking his head in disbelief.

"So, you want me to believe you're a human named Sara Slick who was trained by these Farsiders, and you're investigating all this because you think it might be connected to some guy named Hobbes who wants to end the world?"

"Essentially, yes." It was the Reader's Digest version, but it was something.

"I thought," he put his hands on the table and looked at me with the sternest expression he could manage, "we said no bullshit."

"I promise you. There was a minimal amount of bullshit there."

"I just... That's insane. Everything you told me is insane. Why would I believe it?"

I reached down into my pocket, and in one motion, deposited Splinter on the floor. He scurried around for a second, then ran back up my leg and settled on my shoulder.

"May I introduce Splinter?" Jonas was no longer moving, his eyes wide and focused directly on my furry friend. "Splinter, go get me a pen and paper, will you?"

Splinter happily hopped down off my shoulder, ran up

the leg of the desk Jonas sat at, crossed directly in front of his folded arms, and grabbed his pen. Looking up at Jonas for a second, almost seeming to dare him to say something, Splinter grabbed a sheet of notebook paper out of a notebook on the desk. As he tore it off, he maintained eye contact with Jonas. Then he ran back to me and deposited them both in my hand. I wrote three words on the paper and handed it to Jonas.

"Believe me now?" he read back to me. "I don't know, Sara."

"Slick. People call me Slick."

"Slick. I don't know. Either you have the most exceptionally trained rat I've ever seen, or there's some kind of magic at play. Frankly, I have no idea how to tell the difference. I guess I'll believe you."

It wasn't a resounding win, but it was a win nonetheless. Now I could get back to my original purpose of getting help for finding Ally.

"I'll take it. Now, as for Ally," I began.

"Right. What can we do?"

"We can't do anything. I need you to help me by telling me where you think the Vrya compound is. If I can find where they are, I can get her back. The Vrya are a group of dryads. I've fought creatures like them before, and with a little luck and the element of surprise, I think I can get her back."

He slowly nodded. It seemed like he wanted to argue, but he was out of his element, and he knew it. Instead, he took a moment, then put one finger in the air like he thought of something. He stood and turned to a cabinet behind him, then rummaged until he pulled out what looked like a long, laminated piece of paper.

"I do a fair amount of hunting in these woods. Everyone around here does, but I enjoy getting out there and exploring while I do it, and I have noticed a few odd things." He put the paper down on his desk. It was a giant map of the town and the surrounding area, but it was hand-drawn. It looked like the town and some of the outskirts were traced from an official map, but then the forest itself was all done by hand by a patient and extremely thorough person. Quite a lot of the woods were mapped out, but there was a giant section near the middle that wasn't.

"Who drew this?" I was amazed by the detail. "It's impressive."

"I did," he responded, not letting the compliment get to him. "Now, the terrain in this area where it's blank is really difficult cliffs and thick underbrush. Without proper equipment, it might be tough to get around, and I've mostly avoided it in favor of exploring easier-to-traverse areas. But, as you can see, I have explored almost all of it, except for this area here." He pointed at the map. "If they have a place out there, it would be here."

"Can I take this with me?" I asked.

"Sure. I have copies. Just remember, this terrain is challenging, even for someone experienced with it. Bring supplies with you in case you might need to stay out there awhile." He handed me the map.

"That's fine. I'm about to go hunting there. Plus," I tucked the map inside my jacket, "I know a thing or two about surviving."

CHAPTER TWENTY

I tried to keep myself calm as I marched deep into the woods, combing the area I explored with Ally and heading toward the mark on the map. It wouldn't do any good to get overly upset or vengeful or emotional about them taking her. All it would do is make me less focused and possibly get one or both of us killed.

I needed to be vigilant, and I needed to be clever if I wanted to get her back safely and get out of there alive. I knew what it was like to fight dryads, and what I was in for was not a fight I looked forward to.

Leaves crunched underfoot as I crested the hill leading to the clearing where they snatched Ally. A lump formed in my throat as the thought of them hurting my best friend ran across my mind, but I tried to shove it down. Deep down. I couldn't let it affect me, not if I wanted her back. I had to approach this like any other mission, any other situation, and let my senses and my instincts guide me. If I thought too much, I could jeopardize everything.

I closed my eyes for a moment and tried to shove the

thoughts filling my mind away. After breathing a long, slow breath out through my mouth, I opened my eyes and set my focus slightly beyond the clearing. According to the map, there was a barely visible trail there, and it would lead to a dense area of the forest.

There was a natural pathway there, but downed trees, thick brush, and hundreds of tiny streams populated it. It was hell to traverse, which was why Jonas hadn't yet done so in the search for what was out here, but I was determined that I would. I sipped the water in my flask and screwed down the top, then hung it back on my belt.

The belt was new. Archie suggested it when I told him what happened and where I was going. Having a few supplies on me in case I ended up lost or wandering in the woods for a few days wasn't the worst idea in the world, and a belt was easy to shed if I ended up in a fight and needed the freedom.

A few other supplies were tied to it, or in various pockets, and it made me feel a little more confident. No matter where this place was, I was prepared to stick it out until I found it. It even had a pocket for Splinter. Granted, it was supposed to be a pocket for something else, but Splinter fit so nicely in it and loved being rocked to sleep on my hip so I couldn't take it away from him now.

As I entered the wooded area beyond the clearing, it seemed like the world got darker and more sinister. The trees were lush and thick and covered most of the sunlight, so it only came down in jagged patches on the leaf-covered ground. The trail, such as it was, led a winding path deep into increasingly taller trees. I followed it, occasionally looking down at the map to mark my progress with a pencil.

I wanted to follow a direct path north through the woods first, right through the middle of the area Jonas said he had yet to explore while hunting. Then I could double back and cross it going east-west. If I explored the area in sections, always going in one direction, I could keep myself from getting too lost.

As the woods enveloped me and the trail all but disappeared under my feet, I put up the first of my markers. A stack of yellow paper I brought for the occasion, a few dozen nails, and a short hammer were my way of creating landmarks. I hammered the first paper in, drawing an arrow pointing south to the trail and kept going north.

Once the trail ended, the terrain got heavier, craggier and more difficult. Streams so small I could step over them in normal stride now gave way to ones requiring me to swim to get across. Hills that took only a few running steps to get up easily gave way to rock faces spanning for miles and required me to climb them to keep going. I was getting very close to the area Jonas had pointed out on the map. Only a mile or so away, and I would be there.

To whatever fight was waiting for me. If I couldn't sneak in and escape with Ally, I would have to punch my way in or out or both. That could get tricky. I fought dryads before, back when I was in The Deep. Two of them. The Twins.

They arrived in The Deep about halfway through my stay and immediately caused havoc. They were big and dumb and brutal and fed off each other's anger and hatred. Differing in size and shape from the tall, lanky ones that took Ally, these dryads were shorter and stockier with thick, round heads and ham-hock hands.

They could club you to death with them, and often-times, that was their favorite means of malicious mayhem. Their bark was dark, almost like it was wet and covered with mold. Grabbing it did nothing since it broke off easily and fell to the ground like driftwood. They beat other pris-oners for nothing, just for fun, and targeted me one day because they thought I looked like an easy fight. They made a terrible mistake that day.

Solon had visited me earlier, and I felt sharp and hungry and ready for a fight when they came to me. They tried brute force, and if I hadn't been trained and already tough from surviving as long as I had, they might have killed me right then. But I fought back, used their weak-nesses against them, and killed them both.

The first had the unfortunate experience of being set on fire. Once a dryad began to burn, it was almost impossible to stop it. When he went up in flames, his brother panicked and tried to put him out. He grabbed a leaky bucket that some prisoner had put out to collect water dripping from the damp ceilings, and then tried to bring it to his brother. But I kicked the bucket as hard as I could, and it saturated him.

Dryad bodies soak up moisture quickly, and for a short time their bodies are so full of water it becomes easier to cut into them. I used that opportunity to slice his neck with the switchblade, and he died shortly after. As he died, he tried to crush me by grabbing me and squeezing me to death. He clasped my leg and squeezed hard enough that I likely had a shin fracture.

That was then. I wasn't nearly as well trained as I was now, but there weren't nearly as many dryads as there were likely to be here. There were at least a dozen of them when they took Ally, and although I had zero problems setting every last one of them on fire and dancing in the flames, saving Ally was far more important. I did promise myself that whatever they did to her, I would return to them twice over. That was enough.

Splinter climbed out of my pocket to scramble up the rocky cliff face before I did. He was good at that, and if something were waiting for me up there, he would either tell me or not come back. Either way, I would know to be careful. He was gone quite a while when I heard him squeak fairly far off. He had found something, but it wasn't his 'immediate danger' squeak. I climbed up as fast as I could and followed him.

He was sitting behind a tree and peering through the branches. There was a brush of trees bending inward like an entrance, and two dryads guarding it. I need to get in there and see what they were guarding, but first, I needed to neutralize them. After sending Splinter along to one side, I picked up a rock and threw it in the other. One of the Vrya guards noticed the sound and went to investigate. That would give me and Splinter the chance to pull a trick we'd tried before.

Splinter ran toward the remaining dryad. Rather than screaming or yelling, the Vrya bent down like he was greeting a dog. Splinter leapt in the air and jumped onto the dryad's face, chomping away at his bark-like skin. As he did, I came around and behind the guard and pulled out a small ax I brought for the occasion.

I sank the ax into the dryad's knee. Before he could cry out in pain, I wrapped his mouth with a bandana, then pulled him back toward me and slammed his head onto a nearby rock. He fell unconscious. Maybe dead. Either way, I wasn't going to cry about it.

I could try to sneak in now, but I knew the other guard would come back, see his brethren knocked out or dead, and sound the alarm. Instead, I went after him and found him with his back to me in the woods while looking for the source of the sound caused by the rock. I grabbed a large rock from the edge of the entrance and hoisted it over my head. Sneaking up on the dryad as quietly as I could, I made it to just behind him as he knelt looking for any sign of someone in the woods. I brought the rock crashing down on the back of his head, and his body sank to the dirt.

Splinter hopped onto my leg and climbed into his pocket again as I made my way to the entrance. Hopefully, it would be a while before the shift change, and I would have a chance at finding Ally and getting out before those two woke up. If they ever did.

"See, Splinter? No locket, no problem."

Splinter didn't respond. Impressing him was harder than impressing Solon, sometimes.

CHAPTER TWENTY-ONE

I had no choice but to go through the opening but knew I should find a way to hide as soon as possible once I got close to whatever kind of encampment the Vrya had. By the sound of it, it would be a fairly large one, which might work in my favor. If there were a lot of them, it might be easier to hide since they would be distracted by one another.

Of course, I'd have to be more careful about moving, but I was pretty good at that already. Years in The Deep taught me how to stand so still I seemed like part of the scenery, and if these things were as vicious as it seemed like they might be, I would need to be extra scenic.

The entrance led down a gradual decline, and halfway down a road appeared under my feet. I almost didn't notice it, but when I did, I marveled at its craftsmanship.

It was solid, but felt almost a little springy, like rubber, but camouflaged with dirt and what looked like intricate paintings of local flowers and grass. It was also set into the ground, so it didn't raise and change the elevation, despite how it wound over hilly terrain. I tested this by stepping a few feet to the side and feeling the solid ground, then stepping back on the path. It was so cleverly hidden that I wouldn't have noticed it had I not stepped onto it.

While the pathway was impressive, it was nothing compared to what I saw when the tree line thinned and the world spread around me. I ducked behind a massive oak right before I walked out into an area with no trees.

I had almost wandered out into what was essentially a clearing but was dotted by tall standing trees reaching high into the sky and marking an entrance point for those who knew it was there. Beyond were smaller trees, thousands of them, with vibrant green plumage on top that fell in bowl shapes over what they hid beneath.

Every tree had a building of some kind built around it. Some looked like homes, some like stores, some like offices, but they all shared one thing in common—the trees. A few of them looked like they took up several trees for one construction, and I imagined what kind of space it must be inside. It was incredibly impressive but eerie.

The entire area was empty. Not one dryad walked around. No business was being conducted, no children played. Everything was still and quiet. I checked my pocket for the secret weapon I packed for a fight, in case they were lying in wait. I knew if it got down to fisticuffs, I could probably handle myself for a little while, but eventually, I would need to break out the big guns. When that happened, I needed to be ready, and with my secret weapon, I had as good a shot as any.

On the other side, in the pocket on my hip, Splinter sat with his little hands on the edge of the pocket, his face peeking out. He was more than happy to accompany me and be an extra set of eyes, but it didn't seem like he was particularly a big fan of running around an empty Vrya village by himself. I didn't blame him. This place was giving me the creeps.

I snuck behind one of the buildings and tried to peek inside. The bottom of the windowsill was too tall, and I had to reach up and do a pullup to see what was going on inside. When I got up there, though, a curtain had been drawn and the room was dark. Trying a couple more windows around the house provided the same result. I finally found one that didn't have a dark window, but a lighter one, nearly clear to allow in light.

It was a store, and the door had a wooden "CLOSED" sign up. It looked almost like a pharmacy, with shelves of bottles of different ointments and liquids and bandages, and in the back, there was a long bar. A machine stood on one side of it, and I suddenly realized it was a soda machine.

This was an old-school pharmacy like the ones in the TV shows my father used to watch about the fifties. It looked quaint and adorable, but still new. It was as if coming into this town not only transported me to a world full of Vrya homes and businesses, but also to a different decade altogether.

I hopped down from the windowsill and made my way behind the next building. This one was long and higher than the others, with stairs rising to both a front and back door. Deciding to press my luck a little, I climbed the back steps as quietly as possible. Peering in the door, I saw what looked like three rooms, each one with a door open to reveal an office. A lobby area was on the front side, and a hallway between the rooms led to the door where I stood. The dryads who lived here were not only surviving, they were living mostly normal lives, but in a small commune of their kind. I didn't know how I felt about that. My instinct was to distrust and fear Farsiders and dryads especially, but this didn't look like the work of evil beings. This looked like the work of beings who wanted to get along. Perhaps the Vrya weren't like the other dryads I had known before.

But they kidnapped Ally. And knocked me out.

There was that.

From this vantage point, high up, I saw a building in the center of what constituted a town for the dryads. Everything else was so expertly hidden from above that this building seemed conspicuous. A plane flying overhead wouldn't see anything out of the ordinary with the area, but a structure that big they might. Then I noticed the roof, which was painted brown and had more of the intricate artwork from the pathway.

I climbed down the steps and snuck my way to the main building. There was a faint murmuring sound here, and I quickly ducked behind a wall, narrowly avoiding being seen by a Vrya guard. I peeked around the structure and saw there were two of them, but at the moment they were both preoccupied with having a conversation I couldn't hear in a far corner.

The murmuring wasn't coming from them, however. It came from inside the building. A voice, loud and booming like thunder rang out in laughter, and I steeled myself. A person who laughed like that was a person who threw their weight around. In a small community like this one, that laugh indicated a person who would know what had happened to Ally.

I took the opportunity of the guards being busy to sneak around to the front of the building. I could tell there were several Vrya in there by voice and movement. I counted individual footsteps around the room without looking in, only listening to sounds too far apart to be one walking subject. I counted five, but that was a minimum. There could be more.

Good thing I brought my secret weapon.

Not yet, though. That was last. First, it was time for some good old-fashioned fighting. I placed my hand on the doorknob, an ornate brass circle on the dark, stained wood, and turned it slowly. The faintest of clicks of the door unlatching was my cue. I swung the door open and darted inside, heading for the direct middle of the room. The laughing, booming voice had come from there, and I saw as I ran that it was a portly, older dryad. I flew through the air, my leg muscles responding so well I barely felt like I put any effort in, and flung out a kick that landed directly on his jaw. He flew backward, crashed to the floor, and rolled over himself to sprawl out.

Before they could gain any sense of what was happening, I attacked two of the other dryads in the room, letting loose a punch to one and ramming my knee into the gut of the other. While their hardened bark bodies were stronger and more painful to dole out punishment to, they still felt pain like humans. Granted, it took more to hurt them, but for me that only meant I had to hit harder. I didn't mind hitting harder, especially if the thought of Ally's terrified face fluttered into my mind at any point.

The hard part about fighting any dryad was the height. These seemed to be around seven feet, and I had to leap to make contact with their faces, which often meant my shots were naturally weaker. Considering they were stronger, it meant I had to try to hurt them. Thankfully, these guys seemed like they weren't particularly interested in a fight and the two shots were enough to send them away.

That wasn't true for the other two, who charged me and tried to grab my arm. I snapped it backward in one arching motion and jumped, spinning in the air and thrusting my foot out to connect with the first one's knee. He cried out in surprise and pain as he crumpled to the floor, making his head the perfect height for me to jam my elbow into as I reared back to punch the stomach of the other.

The one-two shot did damage, but not enough. The shot to the stomach of the standing dryad only seemed to anger it, and it grabbed me by the shirt and threw me across the room. I landed with a thud against the wall and tried to stand, moving away barely in time to avoid a kick that would have taken my head off. Instead, he kicked through the wall of the room, and I grabbed a chair sitting nearby and whacked him with it as hard as I could. It exploded on him, and he slumped, his leg still stuck in the wall.

I turned to the first dryad I had attacked, the portly one with the big laugh. He was on his back, his hands behind him holding him up, and he stared at me with a mixture of confusion and disbelief. I pulled my secret weapon from my pocket and showed it to him, and his head began to shake.

"Tell me where Ally is, or I will set this entire town ablaze." I lit the flip-top lighter in front of the squirt gun. The unmistakable smell of lighter fluid leaked out of the tip, and I saw fear cross his eyes.

"You don't understand," he began, and I shot a stream of the fluid at him. His cries of fear proved to me he knew what it was.

"I said... Where. Is. Ally!" I flicked the lighter to life again and held it inches from his face when a voice behind me stopped me.

"Sara, wait!"

I turned in shock. In the doorway stood Ally, and her eyes pleaded with me to stop.

CHAPTER TWENTY-TWO

Splinter was in his element. Several young dryad children scooped him from my hands and brought him down onto the floor with them to play. They rolled a small ball back and forth while encouraging him to chase it. He happily extended his wings, spread out his little fingers, and soared through the air to land on the ball. A few times he got too enthusiastic with it and ended up rolling along with the ball to the next Vrya child. They picked him up and dislodged the ball from his grip and continued. I watched him, a little misty-eyed. I would have to get him a ball for Christmas.

A plate settling onto the table in front of me brought my attention back to the group I sat with. Ally sat beside me as we gathered with a council of Vrya for tea. That was not what I expected. There were many things I might have thought the dryads did with their afternoons, but having tea wasn't one of them.

Oh, well. Learn new things every day. That was the shiny new thing for me to put into my brain for today.

A slightly older woman with the face of a sweet oak offered me a smile as she tipped a teapot over the edge of a dainty cup in front of me. The teacup had a long line down it where it was cracked and carefully mended. It said something about the woman in front of me. She turned to Ally and offered her a bigger smile as she filled her cup with the brightly colored fruit-fragranced tea.

"Thank you, Qulma," Ally said.

I was shocked by the casual, friendly exchange. I had come into the community switchblade blazing, ready to storm the castle and save my best friend. Not only did I not find a castle to storm, but what I did find was a group of perfectly welcoming dryads. Who invited me to tea. And had children who were playing with my pet. I didn't know what to think anymore.

"Are you sure you're all right?" I asked Ally.

It wasn't exactly the most diplomatic or polite question I could have asked, especially considering the plate of cookies being held out to me by the woman she called Qulma. If anybody called me out for it, I would totally blame prison culture.

The truth was, I would have been that blunt before getting kidnapped by the Philosophers Guild. But the dryads didn't know that, and I would milk that excuse for all it was worth. After all, most of the time it was true.

"I'm positive. The Vrya have treated me nothing but well. I have to say, Slick, I think we might have misread the situation."

"What about them attacking us in the woods? I don't think I misread having to fight them and then getting my head smashed into a tree," I pointed out.

"They were defending themselves. What would you do if notorious Farside murderer Sara Slick was walking toward your village?"

I blinked at her a few times. "I mean, I *am* allegedly notorious Farside murderer Sara Slick, so I would probably be concerned about why I saw myself coming for my village."

Qulma jumped in. It was easy to see this woman was the Elder, the leader of this group.

"Ally has told us the truth about you, Sara Slick. And now it's time you learned the truth about us. There are dryads all over the world, but the Vrya have been living together for a long time, trying to exist peacefully. We have no interest in Hobbes or his crusade. We want no part in any of that. We don't want war. All the members of this group have ever wanted was to find a safe place to raise our children. Because of this, we've spent the last centuries as nomads, traveling from wilderness to wilderness, and casting out our kind who caused trouble."

She spoke about the group's travels as though she'd been a part of it, but I knew the dryad lifespan wasn't endlessly long. Somehow, her linking herself to them and creating a single unit of their group, made her seem more real. Her words seemed more sincere, more honest when she spoke about the group like one large family with a continuous thread through them.

"And you ended up in Hunt," I said.

She nodded. "The group settled here, drawn to the quiet and low population. It's easier to cope and stay safe when there aren't too many humans around. For years, we traded with the people in the town. We lived in peace. Then the murders started. We don't know why or who's behind it, but one by one, our people are dying. We hoped it was an accident or misunderstanding, but..."

"I saw the body of the latest victim," I said. "It was no accident."

"That was my fear as well."

Qulma's voice cracked, and she lowered her face, overcome with emotion. It was apparent she was distraught, torn apart by what was happening to her people. I felt for her—for all of them. The pain was so clear, and the broken, tattered bits of my soul still reeling from loss reached out to them.

"What about the earthquakes?" I asked.

"We don't always have control over our power. That's part of the reason we live so far away from others. Strong emotions sometimes bring it out unbidden. Recently, our grief has been so great we couldn't stop it. That's how it started, anyway. After the second and third of our kind were murdered, some members of the community started advocating for retaliation."

A slight shiver rolled along my skin at the mention of them planning to retaliate, but I didn't get much time to think about it. The young man I recognized from the mine jumped into the conversation.

"Why shouldn't we fight back?" he demanded. "They're slaughtering us without remorse. When does it stop?"

"This is Akker." Ally gestured to the young man. "He's...intense."

Her evaluation of him didn't slow Akker down. He glared at each of them, both imploring them to understand what he was saying and daring them to question it or come up with other reasoning.

"The Nearsiders are clearly hunting us. We could bury their town without even trying."

"That's not our way," Qulma rebutted.

I sympathized with him, understanding the wrenching heartache and anger that came from watching people be destroyed and not knowing what to do. The helpless feeling was horrible, and anger soothed it. But that anger was dangerous, and I knew it couldn't be the whole town that was to blame for the murders.

"It's not all Nearsiders. They aren't all like this, and it isn't the entire town of Hunt that is hurting you. I'll help you find who's responsible. And I'll make sure they find justice."

CHAPTER TWENTY-THREE

For the first time in a long time, I woke up before opening my eyes and kept them shut, but not because I was afraid of what I would see when they opened. Not for fear of the clock and how little sleep I got depressing me. I woke up and wanted to lie there without acknowledging the world for a while simply because I was so damned comfortable.

I didn't want to get out of this bed and the luxury of pulling one of the dozen or so pillows under my chest and wrapping my arm around it, then dozing back to sleep was enchanting. My thoughts started to turn back to the nonsense dream that I had slipped out of when another enchanting sensation drove me to open my eyes.

Bacon.

Someone was cooking bacon, and it was close by. The allure of breakfast was the only thing short of an absolute emergency that could get me out of this bed. I reluctantly opened my eyes for the first time that day. The sun was high overhead, meaning I had slept longer than usual, and I stretched, rolling over into yet another impossibly comfortable position I could easily doze back to sleep in.

Laughter rolled into the room from the direction of the wonderful smells, and I recognized it as Ally's. She was already going to give me crap about sleeping in past her as it was. At least getting up now would maybe keep her from the dad jokes.

"Good afternoon," she said as I shuffled into the kitchen, and I checked an imaginary list in my head. Dad jokes were coming, and I had no control.

"It's still technically morning," I said. I was right, it was nearly ten-thirty, but that didn't deter Ally, who was generally up roughly around noon, and was reveling in being up before me.

"Sure, sure." She flipped a piece of bacon on the stove and grinned like an idiot. She was enjoying this. "Technicalities."

The dryad woman in the room with her was busy beating eggs in a bowl beside her, seemingly not wanting to get involved in our snipping. Ally wasn't about to let a partner get past her in this moment of glory, though. She nudged the dryad woman, who looked up at her with an innocent expression.

"Hmm?"

"About what time do you think it was when I came in to help you?" Ally asked.

I was expecting her to say something ridiculous but laughed out loud when I heard her response.

"Oh, about twenty minutes ago," the dryad said. Ally crossed her arms over her chest and nodded primly while working hard to conceal the smile behind her lips.

"See, Slick? Twenty whole minutes before you. Downright perky."

We both laughed, and she turned to work on the bacon again, barely saving a few slices from catching on fire. It suddenly occurred to me how much different an incident like that would be here with the Vrya than to us at home. A little grease fire here was cause for mass panic. Good thing Ally wasn't going to be trusted to cook much.

"Did you sleep well?" The dryad had a soft smile and a pleasing voice. I was damn sure she was an excellent cook, too, by the smell of it.

"Best sleep I've had in a while. Thank you for all this. You didn't need to."

"Oh, I don't mind." She dumped the eggs into a skillet beside Ally and scrambled them with a spatula. "It's been so long since I've had anyone to cook for, It made me happy to help you out."

"I really do appreciate it. The bacon smelled amazing." I noted there was also bread to toast, sausage sat next to the skillet, and there was a wide assortment of juices on the counter. The middle-aged woman moved around and placed a glass by my side.

"I used to cook all the time for my family. I was up every morning right after dawn to make breakfasts not unlike this one, but for a hungry husband and two growing boys." She sighed a deep and heavy breath, and I knew what was coming. It didn't make it sting any less. "They were wonderful men, all three of them. I lost them to a battle with some angry farmers when we lived in Montana. They got caught in the hills and ambushed."

"And the Philosophers Guild didn't help?" I asked

"They showed up after the fact and wiped the surviving humans' memories. But it didn't bring my boys back."

"I am so sorry to hear that." I meant it, too. Shockingly, I felt for a dryad, something I would never have thought possible. But this sweet woman's story was heart-wrenching, even without her going into too much detail. It was apparent how much she loved and missed her family, and the thought of her tooling around now by herself, so happy for us to visit so she could make a big breakfast and remember her boys, it got to me.

Her response was to smile and pour me a glass of orange juice before turning back to the pan Ally was busy scorching the bacon on and turning the heat down. Our conversation left the weightier things and drifted into a comfortable back and forth, with me reminiscing about pancakes and Ally explaining how her grandmother made the world's greatest casserole.

I neglected to talk about tacos, although I was fairly certain if I said anything about them, this sweet woman would have made me a dozen or so to take with me. Instead, I let the conversation drift to topics of entertainment and joy and more stories of her husband in better times. The more I listened to her, the more I realized I thought more highly of this dryad than the vast majority of human beings I ever met.

I finished everything on my plate for a second time and pushed myself away from the table in the international symbol for 'I am so full I might die.' Ally was sipping on a juice cocktail, and I had joined the little lady in helping clean up when the door opened, and Akker walked inside.

The young and angry Vrya seemed less fiery than the day before, but still put out. He walked into the room as if it were perfectly normal to wander in and hugged the woman from the side.

"Oh, Akker, you good boy, would you like something to eat?" she asked in what might have been the most adorable grandmotherly way of asking anything I ever heard. The words practically dripped with the love and attention of a woman with heart to spare.

"No, thank you. I have to get these two going. It's my job to take them into town." He indicated Ally and me. There was a small trace of pride in this announcement. Even if he didn't trust us, or wasn't happy about the assignment itself, the fact he was entrusted to do it seemed important to him. I wondered if it meant maybe he would soften a little on our trek back. Otherwise, if he were like he was yesterday, it would be a long and quiet trip.

"Then you need to pack something to go with," the older lady said in the tones of someone who wouldn't be denied. I got the feeling anyone who came by her house at anything resembling a mealtime ended up walking away with more than their stomach could carry in one sitting. I wasn't about to complain, however. The food was delicious. A few moments later, we all had sandwiches wrapped in plastic on our person and a fat smooch on the cheek to send us on our way.

As I left the older woman, I turned back to wave at her, wondering if I would ever see her again. But she was already inside, busy doing whatever it was that needed doing now that her home was empty again. I suppose if I lost my family the way she lost hers, I might not ever wave goodbye to anyone either. You never knew when it really was the last time. It was easier not to put that finality on it, but to let the moment linger.

CHAPTER TWENTY-FOUR

As we walked to the edge of the town, Akker stayed mostly silent, as though guarded and upset. But once we were out into the woods, he seemed to relax, and I decided to try to get him to talk to us. I was impressed with how Akker respected his elders, despite his apparent wishes to be more forceful with humans, and frankly, I understood it. My prejudices against Farsiders had taken a bit of a beating in the time I spent with the Vrya.

"Do you mind if I ask how old you are, Akker?" I hazarded.

Getting him to talk about himself might go either way. He could be like most men and be all too happy to talk about himself for long periods without stopping to breathe, mostly stories of prowess or toughness or intelligence. Or he could completely shut down, and the rest of our walk would be in complete silence.

Considering the sound of nature in the woods was pretty soothing, and I had spent a decade with no one to talk to but Splinter, and occasionally Solon at random intervals, silence wasn't exactly a disappointment, either.

"Fourteen. It's why I'm so small."

I stared up at him in dumbfounded silence for a moment.

"Small? You must be seven feet tall," Ally said.

"I wish. I'm only six-eight. Most of the men in the village are at least seven feet, but I haven't grown all the way yet. I might be bigger than them." He smiled. He was hoping for north of seven feet.

"From way down here, you guys all look about a hundred feet tall," I said, and he grinned at the ground, where his eyes stayed eternally focused. We reached the craggy cliff wall, and as I prepared to climb down, Akker simply jumped. He landed on his feet with a bit of a thud fifteen feet down and looked up at me. Slowly, he held out his arms.

"If you want, you could jump down. I will catch you."

Ally shrugged. "What the hell? Why not jump into a teenage tree-man's arms from almost twenty feet in the air? Adventures, right?" She dove off without a second thought, and Akker caught her easily.

"Here I come." I stepped off the cliff face and fell sideways. Akker caught me with ease and sat me gently on my feet. "Don't get to do that every day," I said. Akker turned away sheepishly, then continued toward the main path.

"The terrain here is difficult for humans, but for us, it isn't so bad. We've lived in worse places, or so I've heard. Here is the right amount of seclusion and closeness to a town that we can survive easily. Or at least, we did until the violence started."

The sadness and anger in his voice when he talked of the killings was strong. I felt for him. He was a kid and was dealing with terrible realities while trying to swallow the deep call for vengeance. I could relate to that well.

The difference was, while I was trained quite well by Solon and had magic runes fairly often to help me, Akker and the men of his tribe were very physically imposing and strong. I barely got the upper hand when fighting them, and I had the element of surprise and a plan to get what I wanted quickly. Akker looked like his body was made of muscle, and as large as he was, the likelihood was that anyone wishing to fight him would immediately have a rough go of it.

"I know that must be hard. I appreciate you taking us into town."

"Sure." He stepped over a small creek in one stride that I had to take a couple of wide steps to get through. "I go into town fairly often now. I won't be able to soon, and I wanted to get my fill of it before I can't." He noticed me looking at him quizzically and before I had a chance to ask, he answered. "Did you notice the older folk, how their skin is rough and tree-like? That will soon happen to me—it's part of aging. Once we get the bark growing on our skin in places we can't hide with clothing, we have to retire to the community. The children go into town for us, and we are taught very early the value of money, the value of trade, and how to speak with Nearsiders. Our children, even very young ones, can pass for young adults to humans."

"How young?" Ally asked, fascinated.

"I went into town for the first time when I was only five. My mother sent me there to get seeds for something she wanted to grow. Tomatoes or something. Anyway, I was trained for it since I can remember, and she handed me money and told me I needed to join another older boy who was going into town to get her things. The older boy would look out for me."

"That's nice," I said.

"It was. He was." I didn't miss the past tense in his reference. I decided to leave that alone for now.

"So how long do you have before you can't go into town?" Ally tried to change the subject.

"A few months, I would guess. My bark is already coming in on my chest and arms. Soon it will appear on my face and neck, and then I have to be done. I never know if I will wake up one day trapped forever in the woods." Despite his animosity toward Nearsiders over the murders, he seemed to enjoy going into town. I decided to ask the question that had bugged me for a while.

"So, what were you doing in the mine?"

Akker got very quiet for a moment as we continued to walk. He wasn't avoiding talking, but I could tell he was trying to put words to his thoughts, and it wasn't coming together for him. Whatever he wanted to say was very difficult for him, and it started to dawn on me.

"I caused it," he said quietly. "I caused the collapse. Qulma is my mother. The man who was in the mine, the last victim...that was my father."

"Oh." I didn't have better words, not yet.

"I didn't tell my mother I caused the cave-in. I still haven't. I don't think I will. I don't know what else I'm supposed to do. The humans keep murdering us, and I can't sit by and let it happen."

I was about to say something, words to soothe him or to encourage him to look deeper before resorting to violence when he suddenly stopped, his eyes straight ahead and his body still. We had arrived at the clearing where Ally was taken, and something seemed very wrong.

"Fae," I said.

I knew it. As they stepped out of the safety and concealment of the trees and into the clearing with us, Akker spun to look at them all. There were six of them, and a few carried blunt weapons.

"Lovely day for a walk. I'm sure the night will be nice, too. Too bad you won't know," Naida said mockingly.

"How the hell do you keep finding me?"

She smiled. "Let's just say one of your enemies has become one of my friends."

I thought about that for a second, but it didn't narrow it down. I had a lot of enemies.

"Well, if you don't piss off now, my number of living enemies is about to shrink," I shouted.

Akker struck a fighting stance, not unlike a boxer, and I reached for my back pocket. My switchblade was going to get some action really soon. Ally stayed between the two of us.

I expected more repartee, at least something resembling wit, but they attacked instead. I had to admit that it was a sound strategy and one I didn't see coming. One of the Fae tried to grab me from behind, but I went low while kicking backward and connecting with him, sending him slumping to the ground holding his middle. Another reached me in time to catch a slice from the switchblade, then a right cross from Akker that filled the entirety of my vision as it came across me and into the Fae's jaw. It cracked loudly, and the Fae dropped, out cold.

Two more Fae jumped at Akker, one on his back and the other on one of his legs. He flipped the one on his back to the ground and kicked the one on his leg into him, sending them both sprawling. Another dove at me and I ducked, and he landed in Akker's waiting arms, who lifted him over his head and tossed him yards away. Naida smirked as the Fae groaned and tried to stand around us. I leveled a kick at one, sending him back to unconsciousness.

I reared back with my switchblade, daring the leader to attack, but instead, she turned and ran for it, disappearing into the woods in a direction I didn't know. I was about to start after her when Akker shouted for me.

"Slick! Look," Ally shouted and pointed south.

Smoke was filling the woods, and it was coming from the direction of town.

CHAPTER TWENTY-FIVE

We heard the sounds of chaos coming from the town of Hunt while we ran through the woods as fast as we could. People screamed and shouted at each other as the smoke thickened around them, choking out not only the ability to breathe but see. The dark gray smoke billowed in large clouds that seemed to follow one another, making it impossible to orient ourselves reliably. Ally ran right beside me, but Akker got ahead of us, his long legs letting him cover more distance with less effort than Ally and me.

As we left the woods and entered the outskirts of town, I pulled the neckline of my shirt up over my nose and mouth to filter some of the smoke. The worst part was my eyes stinging, and for once, I almost wished I wore glasses. Anything to act as a barrier between my eyes and the acrid gray wall of heat and ash pummeling me.

I called to Akker, but as we entered the town, he ran off faster, presumably to help someone. Ally kept close to me as we followed the road, what little of it we could see, toward the center of the town.

The road led to a hill that went down into a small valley, and through waves of smoke, we saw the source of the chaos. The bar—or rather The Bar—was on fire, flames shooting out impossibly high, and several other buildings nearby were catching. Ally tried to keep up as I tore off toward it. Shailene's voice could be heard over the chaos, directing people to safety and pleading with people to hurry. I ran past her in a bound, and she spun toward me, sputtering as she tried to get my name out to tell me to stop.

My main concern wasn't the bar itself, but the buildings next to it. They were mostly apartment buildings, and the people in those rooms could be trapped inside. Indeed, as I drew near them, I heard crashing windows and screams for help. I made a mad dash for the closest one to me and reached up to grab the doorknob. It burned my hand, but I spun it anyway, noting that for a closer building I would want something to turn the knob with.

Coughs filled my lungs, and I nearly fell over trying to breathe. The smoke was thick and vicious as I banged on the doors of the apartments inside for people to get out. The first apartment door opened as I moved on to the second and the person inside, apparently woken from a nap, stared wild-eyed around, then took off back inside.

I banged on the second door, but it swung open under my hand, indicating the people there had already left. I turned to see the first apartment's tenant hopping out the door with one shoe on while struggling to put on the other. He was planning on running and wanted to make sure he had sure footing, I guessed. Either that or his new kicks were expensive.

I moved to the next floor as Ally came in behind me and started whaling on the other two doors below. Three of the apartments seemed empty, or the doors were ajar, but the fourth, the one closest to the bar itself, stayed closed. I was about to say to hell with it and leave it alone when I heard a faint cry from inside. A baby wailed, as much as it could while coughs peppered its cries.

I reared back and kicked the door as hard as I could, but it didn't break open. The apartments here were old but well built, and the doors weren't the type to be easily knocked down. Thankfully, I had a fair amount of experience with kicking things in, so I tried again. This time, I felt the door split near the lock. One more should do it. I took a step backward and ran at it this time, putting my foot into the weak spot of the door in a Yakuza Kick that focused all of my body weight and momentum on one point. It was more than enough to crash the door open, and it swung in, slamming on the wall.

"Slick?" Ally's frantic voice called from below. "Are you okay?"

"A baby is trapped in here!" I called back down, and she ran up the stairs.

The smoke up here was thicker, but it was hugging the ceiling more. The apartment itself had ceiling fans that seemed to be sucking the air up, and we dropped to the floor to crawl through so we could see better. The crying came from a bedroom almost up against the wall of the bar, and I wondered who would rent an apartment next to the only bar in town with a baby.

We made it to the room, and the door was ajar. I pushed it open, still on my belly, but the door stopped partway. I tried again and heard it thump against something. Ally scooted in and poked her head around the doorframe, and I heard her exclaim something unintelligible.

"What is it?" The smoke made me cough the words out more than saying them.

"It's the mom. She's passed out. The baby is on the floor beside her!"

"Get the baby. Try to wiggle in and get the baby. I'll get the mom."

Ally didn't hesitate, and I was proud of her bravery at that moment. She squirmed inside, and I heard her shuffle around for a moment. "I dragged the mom out of the doorway. Try to open it now."

I pushed the door again, and this time it didn't stop until the entire room was open in front of me.

The walls were on fire, flames dancing up into the ceiling and crawling across the room away from the bar. We needed to get them, and ourselves out of there before it got worse. Ally grabbed the baby, pushed its head into her chest to keep it protected, and stood to run out of the room. I heard her leave through the door when I got to the mom. She was still breathing, but it was labored, and she was unconscious.

Throwing one arm over my shoulder and locking her waist with both hands, I hoisted her to a crouching position, then upright. Then I lifted her again, so she was lying across my shoulders, and ran for the door. As I did, the wall of fire engulfed the room, and the wall to the outside crumbled. I looked back once and distantly saw Akker catch someone jumping from a second-story window in the building opposite. He was so close to the building and the flames coming out of the windows that it momentarily stopped me. It was either an incredibly stupid or incredibly brave thing to do. Maybe both.

I made it out the door and down the steps before a man ran to me and took the woman from me. We all exited the apartment and ran for safety a half a block down. Fire trucks arrived, and citizens of the town threw buckets on the fire and tried to help. Akker was still helping people out of the building on the other side of The Bar, most of them unconscious, and he carried them two at a time. I ran to him to see if he needed anything else, and we turned at the sound of a massive crashing noise.

The bar collapsed, destroyed, and people everywhere were yelling. Akker stood there with black soot all over him, and I realized how dangerous the situation was for him. For a dryad, fire was the worst possible thing to run into, and he went willingly into buildings full of it to rescue people over and over. He might be young, but he was brave. Things calmed down as the fire truck blasted the fire with chemicals and water to suffocate it, and Ally joined me by my side.

"That was brave of you, Akker." I braced my hands on my knees as I tried to settle my breathing.

"I did what I had to do. Besides, dryads aren't as flammable when we're young. The bark isn't old or dry enough yet."

"Still, it was brave of you."

An almost imperceptible redness crossed his cheeks. "Thanks," he said meekly.

A shout from behind me made me flinch, and I realized it was one made in anger and not worry or panic. It was directed at someone. Who, I couldn't tell, but it was full of venom and rage. I turned to see the source of it, and my breath caught in my throat. A mob had formed down the street. Some carried weapons and others shook their fists in the air. They were loud, and angry, and marching toward The Bar, and Cale led the way.

CHAPTER TWENTY-SIX

There was so much noise and chatter among the shouts that I could barely make any single words out until a chant slowly formed. It came from the back of the crowd and rippled its way forward, seeming to infect every person it reached with a violent earworm. They began to chant "KILL THE FREAKS" as one and in increasing volume.

The mob had molded like liquid metal around a small porch The Bar once had for outside seating. Amidst the melted plastic chairs and umbrellas and deformed tables darkened with soot, Cale ran up, turned to face them, and became the voice of their frustration.

His eyes spoke of hatred, and his half-mad smile spoke of malice and self-righteousness. He saw an opportunity to lead a small but destructive force for a means of his own, and he was jumping at the chance, whipping them up first from inside and now from in front.

I saw people like him do this before. It wasn't unlike the fury and devastation Hobbes caused, only Cale was no Hobbes. His big, rounded forearms and stained work shirt made him one of them, one of Hunt. His voice and his life were like theirs, and while he was dumber than a sack of potatoes, he had a built-in sense of belonging and leadership that, in their fury, the crowd went along with.

I strained to hear what he was saying over the crowd's murmuring. They quieted to listen to him, and it struck me how much it looked like a political rally. Cale stood on the platform and slammed his hand on the burnt railing as he spoke, and his words came through, echoing off the still-smoking buildings and in the heads of Hunt's residents.

"The Freak-ahs have been doing this for too long," he shouted. "We were a safe place before. A community where you could leave your doors unlocked at night and send your kids to the store alone and know, *and know* that they would be fine. But these people... No, you know what? I take that back. These *others*, they don't live like we do. They don't care about our safety or our way of life. They only want to take and to cause us pain and destruction."

A collection of the listeners nodded silently, but others shook their fists and cheered loudly at every sentence. Cale was onto something with them and was playing their fears to manipulate them. I felt Akker shift beside me. It seemed his heroism bought him little goodwill.

"Ever since these Freak-ahs moved out here, people have died, jobs have dried up, and more strangers have come around. And I think it's high time we put an end to it!"

Now the listeners being called to action were rumbling and getting more riled. I couldn't tell for sure if he believed everything he said, or if he was using it as a chance to cause violence. Some people only want to hurt. He struck me as that type.

Underneath my feet, the ground started to tremble. It wasn't from the movement of the heavy fire truck, which had been stopped for quite a while, or from the water pumping, which finally ended as the fires seemed under control now. It was from Akker. I could tell he was getting more upset watching Cale, and knowing they were talking about him. His family. His people.

"We should get out of here," I quietly suggested to both of them. "I think things are about to get ugly."

"Why is he saying those things about us?" Akker's voice was full of confusion and anger. "He is lying. That man is a liar, and they're all agreeing with him."

"It's politics." Ally grunted. "Blaming other people for things they think are wrong with theirs. It isn't new, but it is dangerous. Slick is right. We need to get you out of here, but where? I'm afraid if we head back, they'll follow us."

"We should go back to our hotel." I thought quickly. "We all need to go somewhere to rest and breathe clean air. Maybe they'll calm down and this won't turn into anything, but we need to keep an eye on them anyway."

"I'm not leaving until I find out who killed my father," Akker replied as his eyes burned into Cale. The ground rumbled more underneath, and plaster and burnt wood fell from The Bar near Cale, who avoided it and turned a fierce eye back to the crowd.

"God is angry with us for letting these heathens in. We need to do something before it's too late!"

"Come on." I grabbed Akker's massive arm. "Let's go."

The young Vrya reluctantly walked backward a few

steps, his eyes never leaving Cale, before finally turning around and putting his back to him. He walked with purpose but tried to take smaller steps so we could keep pace with him. It was a struggle, but Ally kept to his left and I to his right, subconsciously trying to protect him if someone tried to attack. We got into the hotel room, and I shut the door, then placed my back to it and sighed heavily.

"That man, he thinks we're the problem," Akker asserted, his face a mask of confusion and pain. "I think he's the problem. It is our people who have been murdered. It is our way of life that is being threatened again. Why can't he leave us alone? Why can't they let us be?"

I didn't know how to explain to him that this was so common in human history that my initial reaction was not of surprise but disappointment. The people of Hunt seemed so lovely, but like everywhere else I'd been, all it took was for things to get hard, even a little, and whoever wasn't 'normal' was singled out.

In The Deep that was me, many times. I was the Near-sider, the one who caused all the trouble. No matter if I stayed silent and calm or if I defended myself and eliminated threats to my safety or life, I was the problem. The one to shift the blame to, for everything. My heart hurt for him to experience this so young.

But his youth wouldn't be counted by people who wanted to hurt him. They would see him as a monster and a giant at that. He would be ripped to pieces by an angry crowd of confused and scared people who were led by someone with hate in their heart. There wasn't much time, but we needed a plan.

"Look, we have a ticking bomb here, and it's going to

explode. If they don't calm themselves down, and with a guy like Cale out there running his mouth I don't see that happening, things are going to get crazy, fast. We need to get you out of harm's way," I explained. "We might need to get your family somewhere safer, too."

"Let them come." Akker's jaw set and his foot tapped on the floor as his hands pushed into one another. "I'll take them all on."

"No, that won't help," Ally interrupted. She sat in front of Akker, making him look at her. "Not all humans are like this. I'm not like them. They're scared and angry and confused. I'm sure they'll calm down."

"And if they don't?"

Ally looked at me, but I had no good answer.

"Then a fire is the least of our worries," she replied.

CHAPTER TWENTY-SEVEN

Akker hadn't sat down since we got him into the hotel room. I decided to shower since soot and various degrees of gross from the crumbling buildings still coated me. I didn't bother with the hot water. I had enough heat for the day. The chill of the water soothed my skin and washed away the layer of smoke clinging to me. Looking down at my feet, I watched the water swirl across the shower floor and spin down the drain. The darkened stream looked like the black and white version of *Psycho*.

By the time I got out, all the heat the fire had seared into my skin was gone, and enough chill had gotten to my bones that I shivered my way into the fresh clothes waiting for me on the counter. Adjusting the air conditioner in a hotel from its wintry temperature wasn't my style, so even the air in the room wasn't comforting against the cold. Throwing on my trusty leather jacket seemed like a touch of overdressing, so instead, I tucked myself into bed, resting back on the pillows and pulling the blankets up over my bent knees because I was dignified.

Akker was still pacing. It made me tired to watch him, but I understood what he felt.

"I'm not going to sit by and let these people blame us for these atrocities. We had nothing to do with any of this," he raged.

"We know that, Akker." I tried to comfort him. Or at least bring down his intensity a little. This much anger coming from a towering, powerful young man could be dangerous. The last thing we needed right this second was another earthquake.

He turned sharply to face me. "You heard what that disgusting man said about us. He blamed us for killing our kind and for caving in the mine. Now he's saying we started that fire. He's trying to turn the entire town on us and run us out. Or worse."

"I'd be worried about the 'or worse,'" Ally stated.

"Not helpful, Ally," I muttered through the corner of my mouth.

Splinter scurried off the bed beside me and over to my duffel sagging on the floor. After burying himself in it, he came back out with the remnants of a bag of snacks from the road trip. He stuffed himself into it and came back out with a chip in his mouth. After crossing the room, he hopped up on the second bed, then leapt over to land on Akker's shoulder. He ran down his arm and held the chip out to him. The young dryad looked at the food, then at me.

"He's trying to make you feel better." Tears sprang to my eyes at the gesture from my strange little flying toilet brush rat. "He wants you to have a snack."

184

"That's sweet. Thank you." Akker accepted the chip. Splinter nuzzled him, then ran back over to me.

I shot Ally a smug look. "See? Akker thinks he's sweet."

"I'm working on it," Ally grumbled.

A heavy knock on the door sent Splinter scrambling. He dove under the pillows and stayed hidden while I climbed out from under the blankets and walked up to the door. Akker went stiff, on edge as he stared at the entrance. Nervousness flickered across Ally's face as well. It seemed like each of us was thinking the same thing. Beyond the door could be Cale or more of the mob, ready to drag Akker out and into the middle of the street to turn him over to the rest of the angry townspeople.

"Yes?" I called through the door. "Who is it?"

"It's Jonas. Open up."

I disengaged the chain lock and opened the door. It was only open a few inches when Jonas squeezed his way inside.

"Come on in," I huffed.

"Is everyone all right?" Jonas asked. "Slick? Ally?"

"We're fine," I told him. "It got pretty crazy out there, so we're trying to lay low." I leaned over toward the pillows and shoved my hand under them to grab Splinter. "Come on, you big baby. It's only Jonas."

I pulled Splinter out, and he curled up on my shoulder, trying to hide in my hair. It wasn't a good disguise. Jonas looked across the room, his eyes locking on Akker. The younger man took off his shirt soon after we got here to check a burn across his back. He hadn't put it back on, and now Jonas's eyes scanned over the unusual features of his skin. His gaze moved along Akker's body, taking in his height, then snapped to me.

"He…" He looked back at Akker. "You're a…"

"A dryad," I offered. "It's not a bad word. You can say it. He knows what he is."

"I just…" Jonas seemed so shocked he couldn't even string words together correctly. "The Vrya…"

"Them, too," I confirmed. "That's how it works with families. Generally the same species."

"You conveniently left all that out when you were telling me everything," Jonas said.

"Does it bother you?" Akker asked.

Jonas cleared his throat and shook his head. "No. It was simply a surprise."

"I needed more information before I unloaded everything on you," I explained. "Remember, I said minimal bull-shit. You're the one who gave me that margin. That's all on you."

He held up his hands as if in surrender and smiled. "You got me." The smile faded as he looked around the room at each of us. "So? What now?"

I sat on the edge of the bed and reached down for my boots. After shoving my feet into them, I laced them tightly.

"We have work to do. I need to figure out what Cale is up to and how he plans on executing it. Whatever it is, it won't be pretty, but if I can get to him before he does something monumentally stupid, then I think I can stop a war."

"I'll help you," Jonas volunteered. "I know this area well. I can help you navigate and investigate with you."

I shook my head. "Thanks for the offer, but I need you to hang back here in Hunt. Like you said, you know this place well. And they know you. I need you to try and keep a lid on the mob. Keep things under control as much as you can and don't let them blow up. Do you think you can do that?"

"I'll do the best I can," he said. "But they're angry, and whatever they're up to, they'll get to it pretty quickly. There isn't a lot of time to waste."

"I know. But that's why I need you to hold them back as much as you possibly can. I need some time to unravel things," I told him. "Right now is the time for you to be the very best human you can be."

Jonas nodded. "I think I can manage that."

"Great," I said.

Ally hopped up from where she'd been sitting in an armchair by the window. "I'll go with you. Two people trying to hold back a mob is better than one. And I've been told I can be pretty persuasive."

She smiled, but I shook my head. "You're going to lean into that, aren't you?"

"Hey," she called, one hand landing on her popped-out hip. "I didn't get to be trained by a master wizard and carry around a fancy switchblade and things that blow stuff up. I have to take my strengths where I can find them."

"Fair enough. Go with Jonas and sweet-talk the mob."

Ally grinned and rushed over to Jonas. They said goodbye and promised to keep in touch before leaving. I closed the door behind them and turned back to Akker. He didn't give me a chance to say anything.

"I want to see my father's body," he demanded.

I blinked a few times. "Akker, I know you want to know what happened, but I don't think it's the best idea for you to see him like that."

The young dryad stared at me without a hint of hesitation in his eyes. "I want to see my father, Sara. You got to see him. I deserve to see what happened to him. Especially since it seems some people want to do the same thing to the rest of my family and me. Bring me to him."

He was right. I had seen his father's body, and it was horrific. That wasn't something he should have in his mind. It would stay with him forever, never letting go. But I saw his devastation and anger. He wouldn't give up. I put myself in his place, trying to imagine what it would be like to have something so horrible happen to my father and not be able to be near him. I nodded.

"All right, Akker. I'll bring you. But I have to warn you, it's going to be hard to see."

"I know. But it's harder not to."

CHAPTER TWENTY-EIGHT

"Are you sure about this?" Akker asked.

I pressed my back against the brick of the doctor's office and nodded. "They weren't exactly pleased I gave them the slip. And unless they suddenly got an influx of patients from some other town, I don't think they see enough people regularly to forget my face in less than two days. We can't simply stroll through the front door and ask for a tour of the doctor's office. We have to get inside without anyone noticing us."

"Do you have a specific plan for where we're going in?"

I shook my head. "Not specific, per se."

"A vague plan?"

"Yes."

That vague plan was that we were going to sneak inside at some point. The first time I was inside, I didn't pay attention to other doors or windows along the corridor where we found the makeshift morgue.

It didn't occur to me that I might be back to revisit the body and would need a way to smuggle myself inside. Now

I wished I'd used a little more observation instead of having to scoot myself along the back wall hoping to find a place to get in before getting caught.

Ahead of me, I saw a small metal door set into the wall a few feet off the ground. A metal loop on the side indicated there should be a lock, but there wasn't one. I made my way up to it and grabbed the open ring.

"It's Hunt," Akker said like he was reading my mind. "People don't lock anything around here."

"Well, that's not exactly true."

He looked at me strangely. "What do you mean by that?"

My mind went to the office door and the keypad I destroyed to get in the first time.

"You'll see." I opened the metal door and peered inside. "I think it's a laundry chute."

"Leading to the outside?" Akker asked.

"For the linens to come out to the laundry truck?" I peered back over my shoulder at him. He shrugged, and I climbed into the tube.

"You have to be kidding me. You're not going to try to climb up a laundry chute, are you?"

"I'm not *trying* anything. I'm going to climb up the laundry chute. Remind me sometime to tell you about how I escaped The Deep. Unless there were some severe incidents in a few of the linens sent down this chute, nothing up here is even a close comparison to that. Now, are you coming?"

"Will I fit?"

"Only one way to find out."

Turned out, the answer to that was 'no.' One of these

days, I would need to send a letter of apology to the doctor's office. Then again, maybe not. They were kind of jerks. If they put half as much of the concentration on a fundraiser as they were the whole furious mob thing, they could easily get together the money to fix their keypad and replace the now bashed out of shape laundry chute.

Once I managed to pry Akker out of the tube, we realized we were a floor up from the makeshift morgue where his father's body lay. Doctors chatted down the hallway, and the distinct smell of disinfectant burned in my nose. I shuddered. I'd always hated doctors' offices. We crept out of the storage room where we landed and headed down a back staircase to the floor below.

When we got to the office, I noticed a strip of black tape stretched across the disabled keypad and a new sign hanging on the door that read "Authorized Personnel Only."

It didn't slow us down for a second. Akker grabbed the doorknob, and we pushed into the room. As soon as the door closed, I turned to him.

"Are you sure about this?" I asked. "We can leave right now. Seeing your father this way isn't something you can prepare yourself for. You can wait until they release him, then have a funeral."

Akker shook his head adamantly. "No. He isn't theirs to 'release.' He's ours, and I won't let them decide when or how I see him. I'm sure."

I nodded and made my way to the drawer in the wall. After I pulled it out, I stood in front of the body for a few seconds to block as much of it as possible. I wanted to give the young man a chance to get used to having his father's body out there in the room with him, and to process the reality of it being spread out on a metal table. After a few seconds, he stepped up beside me.

The breath streamed out of Akker's lungs as he stared down at his father. Somehow, the body looked worse than it did when I first saw it. Maybe because it had an identity now. It wasn't only the corpse of a dryad, or a dead Farsider. This was Qulma's slain husband and Akker's father. He was real, with a past and a stolen future. It made it harder to look at the horrible signs of his torture.

"How could someone do something like this to another living being? How could they put him through this?" Akker's hand shook as he reached out and touched some of the signs of the beating his father endured before his death. Suddenly, the touch paused and he leaned closer to get a better look. "What's this? What are these?"

I looked more closely and saw he was pointing at several wounds that stood out compared to the others. They looked strange, and I couldn't put my finger on what they might be. A chart hung beside the drawer, and I picked it up. After flipping through the notes, I found a description of all the injuries. As soon as I read it, I remembered the other times I'd seen those types of wounds. They were scattered across the backs and arms of murderous wood elves who briefly shared my cell in The Deep.

"Arrow holes," I murmured.

He shook his head. "That's no weapon to use underground. He was killed in the woods and dragged to the mine."

"But why? And who? If not the Farsiders, who would do this?" I couldn't understand what we saw. Learning about the signs of murder on the body made the whole situation more confusing rather than making it clearer. "And who would know about the Vrya being Farsiders? It's not like the concept of The Far is widely known. The Vrya are a little less than ordinary, but it's a pretty big jump from that to murder the monsters."

"I don't know, but we didn't do anything to anyone, Far or not. We've been living peacefully and keeping to ourselves. I don't understand why anyone would want to cause any harm to the Vrya, especially to my father."

"It doesn't make much sense," I agreed. "Unless it's part of something much bigger."

Akker suddenly pushed away from the table and stormed out of the morgue. I chased after him, but he was moving so quickly I almost lost sight of him rushing back up the stairs toward the laundry chute. Either the view of his father's mangled, tortured body stretched out with so little dignity or respect on the cold metal table broke him, and he needed a few moments to get hold of his emotions, or his fury had overcome him, and he was out for the revenge he believed he deserved.

Either way, I needed to keep up with him. Now was not the time for him to be alone.

CHAPTER TWENTY-NINE

For someone who had to bend the metal sides of the laundry chute to smash his way into the building, Akker was surprisingly speedy getting out. Of course, me having to fling myself into an open room and hide in the dark with what might soon be another temporary resident of the morgue slowed my pace a little.

Once the doctors passed and the coast was clear, I tipped myself head-first down the chute and rolled out onto the back parking lot. The young dryad was nowhere in sight, but I took off in the direction of town. He was so angry and hurt that I figured my best bet was finding him prowling the people he believed brought that pain.

I was right. I finally caught up with him walking around town, his eyes cutting into the people who dared come out of the buildings. I huffed and puffed my way to his side, wondering if my predominantly taco diet was making a negative impact on my health. One of his long strides equaled about three of my steps, so catching up with him didn't give me much relief.

On the bright side, our little speed-walking expedition was good for my cardiovascular health. I would probably need that for future fights.

"What are you doing?"

"I thought you might like some company. You shouldn't be alone at a time like this."

"I want to be alone. That's why I left."

"First, hurtful. Second, I understand how you feel." My voice softened as I transitioned into trying to comfort him.

If there was anything good I could take out of the ten years I spent buried in the hellhole of that prison, it was empathy. It came with a good dose of distrust and cynicism, perhaps more of a tendency to lash out, and a decided proclivity toward making acquaintances through my switchblade before conversation, but it was there.

"You do?"

I nodded. His pace slowed enough for me to get into a comfortable stride as we made our way down the sidewalk.

"I know what loss feels like. My mother died a few years ago." I paused, thinking over those words and realizing they weren't accurate anymore. I let out a short, mirthless laugh. "I guess it wasn't actually that recently. She's been gone for way more than ten years now. But I still remember how much it hurt to lose her. It still hurts. But you learn to live with it. And it isn't only her.

"While I was in The Deep, I had one friend. Other than Splinter, of course. He was the one who taught me everything I needed to know about The Far, explained how things worked and taught me to survive. He made my switchblade and the tools I used to escape. His name was Solon, and he died before I got out. It was horrible and left me feeling so alone. His death pushed me even harder. I knew I couldn't lose anything else to that prison. Me escaping was something he wanted so much, and I had to make sure it happened for him."

I reached up and rubbed Akker's back. It took a few seconds, but he finally turned and looked down into my face. Emotion misted his eyes, but he gave me a tiny hint of a smile.

"My father was a good man."

"I know he was. He had to be to have your mother as his wife, and you as his son."

"He always wanted the best for all of us. Not only our family but the entire community. He worked hard to give us the best life he could and try to advance diplomacy with the people of Hunt. It cost him his life. But, I'd like to think he would be proud to die defending his people."

Although we still didn't know the exact circumstances behind his father's death, I agreed with Akker's evaluation. Even if he wasn't actively in defense of the rest of the Vrya community when he was attacked and killed, it didn't seem like much of a leap for me to believe it was his actions that put him next on the list for the murderers.

"I'm sure he was also proud of you."

He nodded, his shoulders pulling back and his back straightening with courage and strength. He would fight in the name of his father now, and never let who he was be forgotten.

"Can I ask a few questions about your father?" I asked.

"I would like that. Speaking of him makes me feel less like he is gone."

I had to tread carefully here. There was a kernel of a

theory rattling around in my head, but I needed more information. Perhaps Akker's father was the key.

"Did your father have any enemies that you know of? Other Vrya, or other dryads who had a grudge?" I asked.

"No, my father was well-respected. He was a little stern, but everyone who knew him knew that about him, too. He was always fair."

"He seems like he was a good leader. Did he ever mention anything about the people of Hunt or what was going on?"

"Yes, actually. It ate away at him. My father always felt like the people of Hunt and the Vrya could have a good relationship if they could learn to respect our boundaries and our ways. But the killings seemed to change him. He got harsher when he talked about them, and he spent more and more time in the woods."

"He was investigating." It was a statement, not a question. Akker nodded.

"Even when he spoke poorly of the people of Hunt, he still maintained that something wasn't right, that they were being led astray for some reason. Others in our community thought he was too soft toward them, but they dared not speak up against him publicly."

This time, I nodded. Of course, no one would speak up against him. He was an Elder and a protector. Which meant he was a perfect victim to inspire violence.

It was the kind of thing Hobbes would do.

We had continued to walk as we talked, and I suddenly realized we had ended up near the burnt-down bar. We both stopped and stared at the blackened shell. The acrid smell of the charred building soaked in water still clung to the air. It made my throat burn and my stomach flip. But it also created a new wave of anger that crawled up the back of my neck and tingled in my fingertips and toes.

"I need you to be honest with me, Akker. Do you think your people would have done this?"

There was a chance the question could have offended him and sent him into another rage, but he stayed calm and shook his head.

"No," he said matter-of-factly. "There's no way. Even if members of my community did want to do something horrible to the people in town, they'd never resort to something like this. We hate fire, for obvious reasons. None of us would ever use it as a form of attack."

It was the answer I expected, but it made my mind churn as thoughts tangled and unfurled, repeated themselves, and bounced off each other, all jockeying for position. None of them answered all my questions. There was one thing that was completely obvious to me. It had to have been a human who caused this fire. Why would someone in the town want to create such devastation and fear throughout Hunt? They had gotten the fire under control fairly quickly, but the damage was still expensive. If it hadn't been for everyone working together so closely, it could have wiped out far more of the town and taken many lives. Why would anyone want to do that?

The fire wasn't the only thing to blame on a human. My mind finally settled on the reality that it must have also been a human who committed the horrific murders of the Vrya. Was it the same person? Or were they working together?

Before I had much of a chance to follow that train of

thought or to share it with Akker, I heard my name shouted down the sidewalk. I looked up and saw Ally running toward us. Her eyes were wide, and she looked frantic as she reached for me. Her hands grasped my arm, and she pulled on me, trying to get me to run with her.

"Ally, what's wrong? What's going on?"

"You have to come now. We did everything we could to stop them, but they wouldn't listen."

"What do you mean? What's happening?"

"The mob has gone to attack the Vrya compound!"

CHAPTER THIRTY

"It's chaos," Ally explained through labored breaths as we ran through the town to the entrance of the woods. "They couldn't be talked to. No matter what I said, they kept yelling and getting angrier."

"Where is Jonas?" I rounded the last building and headed up past the mine to the woods where the Vrya lived. The town was empty now, and it was creepy. Some of the houses were left so suddenly that the doors stood wide open. Dogs ran loose in yards, and the air had the smell of gunpowder added to the lingering smoke smell of the fire. It smelled like the beginning of a riot.

"We split up to try to cover more ground. It was a mistake because he got lost in the crowd almost immediately and I couldn't find him again. I went to look for him, but then I realized Cale was gone and people had followed him. One of the stragglers told me they were going into the woods to confront the…" she stopped and looked at Akker, who nodded. "The Freak-ahs."

"Right, the stupid name from the stupid man. If he's

done anything to those people, I swear I'm going to hit him right in his dumb jaw." I wasn't kidding. His dumb jaw had a target painted on it in my mind. One punch might not be enough, though.

Ally looked especially nervous. This wasn't her element, although I suppose nothing that happened since she and I reconnected was really her element. I brought a world of insanity to her life, and she was doing a remarkable job of dealing with it as it came. The violence was getting to her, though, and I knew it. The constant war with the Fae was enough to upset her, but this was something wholly different. This felt bigger than us, and at the same time, I felt uniquely qualified to mediate it and make things work.

I dealt with my prejudices against Farsiders, and still dealt with them, all the time. Farsiders imprisoned me for crimes I didn't commit. If anyone should have a grudge, it was me. But my time spent with the Vrya, and Archie, and even Splinter…it was changing me. If anything, now it was regular people who were pissing me off. Cale, to be specific, was the most colossal asshole I'd met in a long time. I was sure there was one in every town, spread out across time and space.

The one blue-collar guy who the rest of the town thinks is a jerk, but he's so good at bullying and manipulating people to do what he wants, they grow numb to his behavior. Then it gets worse and worse and worse.

Now he was calling them to murder peaceful beings who only wanted to live quietly and without persecution. It was abhorrent, and I needed to stop it. Not try to stop it. I needed to stop it. One way or another.

We were now in the woods and making our way as fast

as we could toward the clearing. Akker was ahead of us but kept stopping to hurry us along. He wanted to get there to help his people, but he knew we were his best hope. If his hood fell off, all it would take was one look at him to notice the markings on his skull, the skin already turning to bark on the back of his head, for them to turn him into a target too.

"Ally," I said under my breath, trying not to alert Akker who was moving ahead of us again, getting to the other end of the clearing and finding the trail. "How many of them have guns?"

"Enough of them," she responded.

"Ally, that's not what I asked."

"What do you want me to say, Slick? This is the sticks! Everybody has a gun here," she exclaimed, but Akker didn't turn around so I hoped he didn't hear.

"We have to talk them down," I said, and Ally laughed. It was a mirthless laugh, but it was something. "What?" I asked.

"Sara Slick, the Farside ass-kicker, saying we need to talk our way out of it. You've come a long way, bestie."

"I might be a Farside ass-kicker, but I don't know if I'm a match for thirty angry dudes with guns pointed at me." I knew full well I would take those odds if it meant protecting the Vrya. "And as tough as the dryads are, no way a fight like this ends without serious death and destruction. Keep an eye on Akker. He'll want to mix it up."

Ally saluted as she ran, and we caught up with Akker, exploding into the woods and heading down the trail. We mostly ran in silence, our ears scanning the countryside for any other sounds, especially sounds of violence. I didn't know if they would find the clearing or be able to get to it, but it took us too long to get here.

We bounded over the last of the obstacles before rounding the area with the craggy cliff. Ropes hung from the top, and the area was torn and beaten like a lot of people had already been there. We were late. The only hope now was that no one had found the actual entrance.

"Come on," I shouted while hopping up to grab a rope and climb. In my near-panic, I flew up the line like every dream I ever had of destroying gym class. Coach Stefanko would be so proud. Or he might yell at me for not having the right form. He was always able to find something he could get you to improve on. Granted, if he saw me literally kicking the ass of a bunch of Farsiders, I think he might have let up a little. Maybe.

Akker climbed the cliff face without needing the rope, and we approached to within a few hundred yards of the entrance in no time. The area was eerily silent. Not even birds or bugs seemed to be making their usual sounds. We blew through bushes and small trees standing in our way from going three across along the narrow and almost invisible trail. Akker was in the middle, though, and a step ahead. I knew that as much as he wanted to get there, part of him was afraid of what he would find.

I smelled smoke now. It was coming from close by. It wasn't the kind we dealt with in the town, the smoke of burning buildings, and fabrics and insulation. This was something more earthy, almost comforting.

Like a campfire.

I pushed myself harder to run faster and leveled with Akker. I knew I should say something before he rushed in and started swinging at the first human he saw. But how do you calm down a seven-foot child?

"Akker, listen, we don't know what we're running into. They have guns and stuff. It could get dangerous, really fast. Maybe you should find your family and get out of here before..."

"No," he cut me off, his voice almost emotionless. "If they found my people and they hurt anyone, then it's not me who's in danger."

CHAPTER THIRTY-ONE

As we cleared the last of the area before the town, the smoke grew thicker, and I felt the heat in the air. Something was burning, and my stomach turned at the thought of what it could be. Images of what I threatened to do, what I had prepared to do when I thought they kidnapped and hurt Ally followed those images, and I steeled myself. I knew how angry and irrational I was then, and I thought I was right. I would have burned them down, every last one of them if I thought they had harmed Ally. I was quick to judge them, and indeed even set one of them on fire, because I let my assumptions push me to a place where violence was my first recourse. Many of these people felt the same. I had to convince them the way Ally convinced me.

We arrived in the town, and smoke filled the air. Men ran toward beautifully sculpted dryad houses, axes in their hands, and smashed them apart. The store I ran behind when I first arrived was in flames but thankfully seemed like the only one so far. It was as if we got there right after they did, and they had yet to cause the worst of the destruction they planned.

"What the hell?" I heard shouted from across the open area of the town. There were a few statues of Vrya there, probably elders of the past or family members. The voice was instantly recognizable, though, even through the smoke. Cale stood in front of them, ax in hand. "What kind of devil-worshiping stuff is this?" he yelled, getting the attention of another man who had a rifle in his hands.

Suddenly, the gun-wielding man kicked the statue, and when it didn't move, he pulled his gun up to his shoulder and shot the head of the Vrya figure. It exploded into dust, and the man cheered. Cale cheered with him, then slammed his ax into another one. They were destroying the memories of the Vrya without knowing what they were destroying.

Out of fear. Remember that, Slick. Fear.

Another man ran to join the fun, heading for the third statue. His ax was high above his head, and he was grinning like a loon. Without thinking about it, I rushed forward, cut him off at the pass, and yanked the ax from his hand. He spun around to me and tried to grab me, not bothering to register if I was a friend or foe, only upset that his violent thought wasn't a reality.

So, I gave him a new violent thought. My fist in his mouth. His teeth—brittle and yellowed by years of chain-smoking and sugar drinking—shattered on my fist and the man collapsed to the ground, a screaming pile of pain. Cale saw this exchange and advanced on me, peering through the smoke to make sure he saw me correctly. I turned to face him head-on.

"What the hell?" he screamed at me as if I'd called his kid out at first when he was safe. "He's one of us, you idiot!"

"You don't know what you're doing, Cale. This has to stop, all of it. Now."

"The fuck it will." Cale squared his shoulders and did the narcissistic misogynist thing men had done so many times when I've told them I would kick their ass, directly before I wiped their smile off their face with my boots. "These Freak-ahs will get what's coming to them. We're going to burn this place to the ground like they burned down our town. Ain't that right?" he yelled to the now-gathering mob.

"They didn't burn down the town, Cale. We don't know who burned what, but even then, it was only one bar and a couple of apartments. No one was hurt." Ally tried to smooth things over. But not even Ally's usual charm worked this time. This time, the person she tried it on wasn't swayed by cuteness, only by fear.

"You don't know anything. You're an outsider, too. Maybe we should burn you with them," Cale spat.

Akker took a step forward. The stoop he always seemed to stand in to make himself look shorter disappeared, and he stood at his full height. His broad shoulders squared, he made eye contact with Cale, and his hood fell to the side and off his head, exposing the bark growing in the back and the markings dryads have. Cale's jaw dropped.

"What the fuck are you?" He pulled a gun from behind his back and aimed it at Akker. "It's one of them Freak-ahs!"

I moved to get between them, but before I could get

there, someone attacked Cale, knocking him over and sending the gun to the ground, where it lamely fired into the dirt. It was a Vrya boy. The dryad mounted him and threw a punch, nearly taking his head off. More came from the woods surrounding us, and fights broke out everywhere. Off in the distance, I saw a man with a rifle, the same one who had shot the statue, have it ripped from his hands and snapped in half before being tossed away like a toy. The man was then also tossed and landed hard on the ground near Cale.

Qulma's voice came from behind me, and I turned to her. Her eyes were pleading, and her hands were outstretched, trying to stop her fellow dryads.

"Please, no more violence," she yelled at them, "it's not our way!"

But many dryads pushed past her and joined the fray, now forming a circle around us. On the inside were humans from Hunt, huddling together and on the outside were pissed off Vrya, prepared to fight for their lives. Qulma joined me in the center of the ring, her hands raised. Near me, a dryad reached out and grabbed a semi-conscious human, and I rushed to him. I yanked the man out of dryad's hands, who turned toward me and swung.

I let instinct take over and dodged the punch, then rapidly trapped it in my arm and spun not only to the side but to the ground. His surprise at my technique was enough to make him lose his footing, and he landed hard on his stomach. I wrapped my hands around his head, tucked his arm in my legs, and used my thighs to pull his arm one way and my hands to yank his neck another. There was a small snapping sound, and I knew I broke whatever counts for a shoulder in a dryad. The creature cried out in pain.

I stood and pushed several Vrya to the side to create a path.

"We have to let them go. They need to go home alive. We will all talk about this later. Move, move!" I screamed, trying to get the humans to see the chance they had. "Get out now, and don't come back. We will talk soon, but for now, take this shot and go! Now!"

It seemed to work. The humans of Hunt weren't prepared for the Vrya to be as huge and strong as they were, and although they were mostly non-violent, the younger ones weren't so calm. Most of those in the inner circle left, and it was down to me, Ally, Akker, Qulma, and Cale. Cale surveyed the group of dryads, then turned his back to the way he came and backed away from us.

When he'd finally gained some distance, he turned and ran out of the town, and disappeared down the trail.

CHAPTER THIRTY-TWO

For several long seconds after the humans ran off, there was no sound but gasping for breath. It was almost too still. It took a young dryad, his face touched by even fewer years than Akker's, to finally break the silence and bring everyone's awareness back to the moment around us.

"What now? What do we do?"

It was such a simple question, but there was nothing straightforward or easy about it. Everyone looked around, hoping to find an answer in someone else's eyes. Finally, Qulma pushed through the row of Vrya closest to me and faced off against her people. Her eyes glowed with anger, and her face looked tight.

"What have you done?" she demanded. "With everything we're facing, you're acting like children. Fighting them like that? You only fanned the flames."

Akker looked at the other dryads around him, then back at his mother. "They were defending me."

The explanation did nothing to calm the older woman.

If anything, it pushed her further into her fury against her people, especially the son she wanted so badly to protect.

"And you. You, Akker. What were you doing revealing yourself to those humans? You know what they think of us. They already had so many suspicions and such distrust for us, and now you've revealed the truth about what we really are. You have to know how dangerous that is. How could you do that?"

Akker's face hardened, his body visibly stiffening at the scolding words from his mother. He did what he thought was right. I knew that. I saw it on his face the same as I saw it in every one of his actions during the standoff with the mob. It was the same type of intense determination and blinding drive that led me into many fights in The Deep.

It wasn't always the best type of motivator and frequently resulted in incredibly unpleasant situations for me, but I understood it. Akker faced the same kind of feeling now. Everything in him pushed him to defend his family and his people. It wasn't only for him. He was fighting in the name of his father now, stepping into the role for him. That type of fuel couldn't be contained, even when it led to actions that might not be the best and could have serious consequences.

"They were going to destroy our town," he pushed back.

The other Vrya around him shouted their agreement. They were still worked up, and their frenzy whipped back up with the reminder of why they joined the fray to begin with. Some of them looked ready to chase after the humans and finish the job. The taut energy and froggy expressions put me on guard. This couldn't continue. Not now. If one of them took off in the direction the humans went, I would have to be prepared to leap on them and pancake their ass to the ground to stop them.

I'd do it, too. I wasn't above tackling a tree person to stop another fight from breaking out.

Qulma shook her head. She wasn't impressed by her son's reasoning or the fervor of the people around them. Much of the anger had drained from her face, replaced by something softer. It was a difficult emotion to describe, somewhere between sadness and love. It was the look parents get when they're so angry at their children for something they did, and yet so overwhelmed by love and pride in them for the compulsion that went into it, mixed with the pain that came from knowing consequences are coming.

"Akker, the town isn't important enough for you to put yourself and everyone else in so much danger. The Vrya people are far more important than the Vrya town. Can't you see that? This place only has one purpose, and that is to keep our community safe and hidden. These aren't ancestral lands. They have no meaning to us except that they have been home, our haven," she explained.

"That's over now," Ally said. We turned to look at her, and I saw tears in my best friend's eyes. Despite the sticky warmth in the air, her arms were wrapped around her tightly like a chill had settled in and wasn't letting go. "There's no way Cale will keep quiet about what he and the rest of the mob saw. He wanted to wipe out the Vrya when he only thought there might be something slightly different about you. Now he knows for sure you aren't human, and he'll crow about it to anyone who will listen. It's not safe here anymore."

Qulma sighed. It was like watching her heart break right in front of me. Suddenly, the dignified leader looked smaller, like part of what held her up and gave her the strength she showed was gone.

"Then it's time for us to move on. Our kind settled here years ago because it was a place where we could feel safe and not worry about threats against us. If that's not the case anymore, it's time to do as our ancestors have done for generations and move along. We'll find somewhere else where we can start our lives again."

I took a step toward her, feeling compelled to stop her. "Maybe it isn't."

"What do you mean?" Qulma asked.

"You heard what Ally said." Akker sighed. "And she's right. Cale won't back down. Now that he has proof of what we are, he won't exist in harmony with us."

There was guilt in his voice. I shook my head, wanting to keep him calm. "That might be true—about Cale. But not everyone in Hunt is like him. I've spent time with these people. They aren't all bad. Maybe there's still time to make things right."

There wasn't the immediate sense of hope I was looking for. If I were sketching out the made-for-TV movie of my life, this would have been the moment when the dramatic music rose and everyone started smiling, and things fell together. Not so much in the made-for-actuality, real-life version I was still living. The people around me didn't look convinced. They didn't even look confident that there was something to be convinced about. Qulma stared at me through slightly narrowed eyes.

"How?" she asked.

"We'll figure it out."

She shook her head. "I won't condone violence."

"I didn't say anything about violence," I protested.

"No offense, but you got your title for a reason. Heinous isn't something they call people known for their loving disposition and ability to bring people together. You aren't exactly known as a peacemaker."

I opened my mouth to argue again, but that was pointless. I didn't live up to my heinous title, but at the same time, I didn't have a track record of handling situations in a calm and non-confrontational manner. It wasn't how I rolled. At least, up until that point. I remembered what Ally said about me still being me, the me before I discovered anything about The Far and was molded into the image of the heinous Sara Slick. I shrugged.

"There's a first time for everything."

CHAPTER THIRTY-THREE

The woods were dark. Ally had gone ahead, trying to make inroads with the townspeople of Hunt while I finished settling the Vrya. Qulma was still suspicious of my ability to bring about a reconciliation, and I didn't blame her. It wouldn't be easy, especially with a loudmouth like Cale stirring the pot.

Ally was the most convincing person in the entire world, though, and having her go work on some of the more influential townspeople might be enough to turn them against Cale and be willing to make this work. Either way, there was no putting the genie back in the bottle. They knew now, and either I would broker peace, or the Vrya would have to leave their home, again.

This had to work, though. It had to. I knew what it was like to be taken from your home, to have to find a way to survive somewhere new, not knowing the dangers, or knowing the hazards and it being life or death constantly. I knew that life quite well, and if I could help it, I didn't want it for the Vrya. At any rate, it could take days for them to pack and leave, and if we didn't calm the townspeople down, they might not have that much time.

These thoughts swirled and pressurized in the center of my head and gave me a mild headache to go along with the stress. Then I heard a branch snap behind me. I had no flashlight and no way of seeing other than the starlight above me and the faint glow of my cheap-ass cellphone.

It was enough to make sure I could see a foot or so in front of me, but it was pretty useless at seeing further than that. So far, that hadn't mattered much since I remembered the trail and the method of getting in and out and was confident I could do it without a light, but I wasn't prepared for random creatures of the darkness sneaking up on me.

I stopped cold, instinctively holding my breath and reaching for my switchblade. It was possible one or more of the townsfolk hadn't left and were waiting to go back in. Or for me to come out. The Vrya had tried quite vociferously to get me to take one of their men with me to the town for protection, but I refused. If I gave the impression that I sided with the Vrya before we could talk, there would be no talking. I needed them to see me as neutral. At the moment, however, I wished I said yes.

Another branch snapped, this one much closer, and I grasped my switchblade. The math in my head blew trajectories and likelihoods and angles at me in instantaneous speed, and I spun, blade in the air, prepared to make a downward strike and roll. But I stopped myself. There in the dark, now only feet from me, was Jonas, his face a mask of surprise and confusion.

"Don't kill me." He crouched backward, hands over his face. I sighed heavily and lowered the blade. Why was he out here in the dark like that?

"Jonas, what's going on? Where did you go? Why are you out here?" I peppered him with questions, and he stood on shaky legs to answer them.

"I came to get you. Ally sent me, and since I've been out in the woods to hunt a lot, and it was dark, I figured it was safer for me to come out here than her. I've been with some of the townspeople, having a meeting. I didn't know you guys were out here until they started filtering back and Ally found me."

"What did they say?" I asked eagerly. Jonas' mouth thinned, and he seemed apprehensive.

"Well," he held his hands out by his sides, "they agreed to meet, but I don't think it will work out too well. They refused to go unarmed. Chances are, there will be some bloodshed before it's all said and done."

I figured. As much as I wanted to patch things up and create peace between the two sides, I had no illusions that it would be rainbows and butterflies. They were highly worked up when they left, and the Vrya weren't much better. I would have to work on them, and it might take time to get them to be reasonable, but I had to try. For the sake of the Vrya, for Akker.

"I know, Jonas. But we have to try to stop a war from breaking out. We are the only thing standing between peace and violence."

Jonas stared at me for a long time. It seemed like he was internalizing what I said, but there was something off about it. Like he didn't believe me or felt defeated already.

"What makes you think there could be peace here?" he finally asked, as we walked back toward town. Despite it being dark, I felt more comfortable with the direction and having someone with me was comforting. "Why would you be able to stop any of it? Why would you want to? You told me about what the Farsiders did to you and those," he paused as he searched for the right word, pointing back to the village of the Vrya, "things, they're Farsiders."

"They are," I was a little taken aback, "but they're good. It's true I had some terrible things done to me by Farsiders. And some horrible stuff was done right back, but in my name. Yet somehow, I'm still alive to talk with you right now. Against all those odds, I'm still here, and one of the reasons is those *people*. I owe it to them to give them a chance."

Jonas' head bowed as if he were thinking extremely hard about what to say. We reached the cliff face, and I noticed there was one rope left. He gestured to it.

"After you."

Something in the way he said it made me pause. There was a flicker of distrust, although I couldn't tell if it was from him or me. Something was strange between us. But he had my back before, and I was running out of people I could put my faith in.

"You understand, right, Jonas?" I picked up the rope so I could lower myself.

Jonas forced a smile and nodded. Some of the distrust disappeared. His smile, while forced, seemed more resigned than disbelieving. Maybe I would need to work on him a little, too.

"I believe Sara Slick can do anything she sets her mind to," he said as I started down the rope. I looked up at him. He was crouched over the edge, holding the line to steady it. The shadows of the forest hid his face, but his eyes shone down on me anyway. "Absolutely anything."

CHAPTER THIRTY-FOUR

This will work. It's a good idea. This will work. It's a good idea. This will work. It's a good idea. This will work. It's a good idea. This will work. It's a good idea.

It was right about that point when I started wondering how many times I needed to repeat my new mantra for it to work. I was relatively new to the whole mantra thing. In fact, it was my first. But it was my understanding that if I said it enough and believed it deep in my heart, it would go out into the Universe and make hope babies that would come down and make all my dreams come true if I clapped. Or something like that. I was kind of fuzzy on all the particulars, but it was all I had going for me right now, so I clung to it.

I was sitting at a large table with Qulma and a few of the Vrya adults. We'd been waiting for more than an hour, and the anxiety and tension built with each passing moment. Ally and Jonas went off to talk to the humans and ask them to come for a meeting. It could be the best thing for everyone involved. It could go horribly. Right then, it was pretty much a crapshoot, and all we could do was wait and hope. Frankly, using my switchblade against drunken goblins was way less stressful.

A hush came over the rest of the Vrya standing behind us, and I looked up to see Ally and Jonas approaching. A few steps behind them came a group of humans from town. Cale and Shailene walked out in front, their faces a study in contrast. While Cale twitched and glared, his eyes like hot coals in his face and his teeth grinding so hard they could crumble into nothing any second, Shailene looked curious and open, willing to find out what we had to say. The two species faced each other across a divide as narrow as the table and as vast as an ocean. I bounced around like a weird little buoy in the middle.

The group of humans stopped in front of the table and stared at us. It was clear they were taken aback by seeing the Vrya and what they truly looked like—an experience I could resonate with. Murmurs and whispers rippled through the crowd and guns poked out from beneath shirts and in back pockets. Lots of guns. That didn't bode well for the whole peaceful talking idea.

There were a few tense moments where it was touch-and-go whether they would stay, but finally, Cale, Shailene, Ally, Jonas, and two other humans took seats across from us. Like the Vrya standing behind us, humans gathered behind the group sitting at the table. There was a stark difference between the group of humans and the group of Vrya, along with me. It wasn't only the large spears that the dryads held poised and ready to use them if they felt the need. It was the individuals who made up the groups. The entire Vrya community was there, including every one of the young children. They represented every aspect of the Vrya, all ages, all points in their lifespan, all elements of what made up their kind. The human group only brought adults. All the children were at home. It sent a message that made the chances of this working out seem slimmer.

I looked at Ally across the table, lifting my eyebrows slightly to communicate with her. This was her chance to use her smooth-talking superhero powers. She nodded.

"Thank you for coming, everybody. We've come together to try to bring understanding and make meaningful progress in the relationship between the humans of Hunt and the Vrya," she said.

A few on either side shifted uncomfortably, but we kept going. Shailene leaned slightly forward.

"What are you people? Are you even people?"

"They're people as much as you are," I told her.

"We are dryads," Qulma answered. "We are what we are."

That drew a line in the sand. She didn't want to get into details about their species, which I understood and agreed with. There was no reason to delve too far and make the situation even worse.

"Are those children back there?" she asked.

"They are."

"How do you have them? I mean, do you plant them?"

I cringed. This could be going a bit less offensively. But at least it seemed like the bartender was catching on, if from a completely wrong angle.

"We aren't trees," Qulma told her patiently. "We bear our young much the same way you do. And as you can see, they look like your children. They play like your children. They learn and laugh and cry and grow like your children."

"But they aren't like our children," Cale snapped. "They'll grow up to be like you."

"And what's wrong with that?" I asked.

He scoffed. "Look at you sitting over there with them like you're one of them. It's disgusting."

"It's disgusting that I don't think we're all that different, and that even if we were, that's no reason to want to wipe each other off the face of the planet?" I asked.

"Why do you live out in the woods?" Shailene asked.

She looked around at our surroundings. The table carved from stone sat in the middle of a clearing given a low-hanging ceiling with thick, richly colored tree branches. Flowers grew like a carpet along the edges of the clearing, filling the air with their perfume. A creek bubbled and danced only a few feet away, creating a soothing sound that brought to mind a sense of life and rejuvenation. It was a special place for the Vrya, a meeting place for peaceful talks and a setting for weddings and celebrations. They'd offered it for this gathering, a gesture of openness.

"Peace," Qulma said. "Our kind have always traveled. We move from place to place to keep our families safe. We chose this place because it felt secure. It seemed like we could build our lives here."

"That's enough of this small talk shit. I want to know what really matters," Cale interjected, shoving himself rudely into the conversation the way it seemed was his general procedure in life.

"And what real shit would you like to know?" I shot back.

Ally snapped her eyes to me, but I didn't care. I'd had enough of this man. In my time out of The Deep, I'd learned I had no patience for kale, and now I knew that turning that 'k' into a 'c' didn't make any difference.

"Why'd these things cave in our mine?" he growled.

Akker didn't give his mother a chance to try to answer. He slammed his hands on the table and leaned toward Cale. "I was distraught. One of *you* had just murdered my father."

Cale pressed his hands to the table and pushed himself up, spitting his way through the first words of an incoherent response. Shailene put her hand on his back and tugged him back down.

"Sit yourself down, Cale. You aren't doing any good acting like that."

"Acting like what?" he demanded.

"Enough." The bartender turned to Akker. "I know my town. Cale and his pleasant demeanor aside, I can't see any of my people doing something like that."

"Well, then who did?" Akker asked.

Qulma was done with sitting aside and letting her son carry the weight of the talks on his shoulders.

"There's time to wrestle with the past later. I'm here to discuss the future. Are our people safe?" she asked.

Out of the corner of my eye, I saw Jonas lean close to Cale and whisper something in his ear. I thought he might be trying to help by talking to him man-to-man. But whatever he said, Cale's eyes darkened. My heart tightened, and my body went on high alert.

"Are our people safe?" he spat. "These freaks can cause

earthquakes with their damned minds. They could level the whole valley."

Behind me, the Vrya were getting angry. The representatives at the table were grumbling at each other and snapping at the humans across from them. Qulma stood and put her hand on Akker's back.

"Go take a walk, son," she told him. He complied reluctantly, still muttering to himself as he made his way out of the clearing. When he was gone, she turned her attention back to the people across the table. "We can control ourselves. Can you?"

Shailene started to say something, but Cale had reached his breaking point. He shot up from his seat and looked around at the other humans.

"Are you going to listen to her? Are you going to believe them? They aren't like us. Look at them. They're nothing but freaks. They're unnatural, demonic monsters who tried to bury me and then came into our town and tried to burn it to the ground. We will never be safe as long as they live so close to us."

He was trying to rile up the others and was succeeding. Things were getting heated, shouts and slurs coming from both sides, angry words getting spat back and forth, and weapons drawn. I stood to try and calm everyone down, but only a shrill, bloodcurdling scream brought a lull to the conflict.

It wasn't me.

An instant later, a young dryad ran into the clearing. "Something has happened to Akker."

"What?" I stepped toward her.

"Somebody attacked him."

CHAPTER THIRTY-FIVE

My stomach jumped into my throat, and I immediately ran after the young dryad. She backed up a few steps as if she couldn't stand being anywhere close to the spot where she pointed. An older member of her community came up behind her and wrapped protective arms around her shoulders, pulling her back against him. I had to guess he was her older brother. It was the same type of gesture I would have used to defend any of my younger siblings if something this terrifying were happening to them.

"That way?" I asked.

She nodded and pointed, waving her long finger frantically. She turned her head into the man's chest, and he leaned his cheek down to rest on hers, creating a shield around her with his body. I didn't have to go far into the surrounding woods to see what terrified her. The sight brought my feet to a skidding stop and made my heart fall.

Arrows stuck out of the trees all around me. Some looked like they were shot just for show, to mark what happened and instill terror in anyone who saw them.

Others weren't as ornamental. Blood clung to the heads of some of the arrows and more spattered the trees and the ground. Ahead of me, I saw a pool of blood soaking into the earth and a narrow trail leading away from it.

A chunk of bark looked torn from one of the trees, but when I looked closer, I saw it shimmer with fresh blood. It wasn't bark, but a piece of dryad flesh. The Vrya and the human townsfolk rushed up behind me, and I whirled around to push them back.

I didn't need any of the humans getting into the area and ruining anything that might lead us to Akker or let us know what happened to him. And I didn't want any of the Vrya coming onto the scene and seeing the horror. Especially Qulma. She had already been through enough with the loss of her husband. She didn't need to know the brutality inflicted on her son.

But it wasn't enough. I couldn't stand in their way enough to stop them. As soon as they reached me, they streamed around me to see what I was looking at. Instantly, the entire group erupted in shouting again.

"Look at this!" one of the Vrya screamed. "Look at what they've done! These people say we're freaks and putting them in danger, but look what one of their kind has done to Akker!"

"Us? What evidence do you have that it was one of us?" a human man shouted back at her.

"Of course, it's what they're going to say," Cale sneered. "These disgusting monsters get off on ripping through their kind and then blaming us. They won't hesitate to start working their way through us."

"None of the Vrya did this." Another dryad squared his

chest against Cale. "This isn't the way of our community. We wouldn't do something like this."

"You think any of us believe you? You're filthy liars. You probably planned this whole ridiculous meeting so you could lure that creature away and do this to him."

"That creature is my son," Qulma shot back angrily.

"I don't care who or what he is. One of your collection of freaks wanted to have us around to see this. They're getting some sort of sick pleasure out of parading around what they did right in front of us. They did it to him, and they'll do it to our children," Cale insisted.

The humans roared, and the Vrya started toward them, but Ally and I managed to stay between them.

"You don't know what you're talking about," a dryad hissed. "Unlike you humans, the Vrya are kind to one another. We don't turn our backs or enjoy hurting each other."

"Don't you dare talk about humans," Cale seethed.

"That's enough, Cale," Shailene said. "You need to back off."

"No. Why should I back off? The good people of Hunt shouldn't have to be afraid of these demons lurking around in the woods outside our town. This is our land, our town. We shouldn't have to worry about the lives of our children. Can you imagine what they would do to them?"

I glanced at Ally, and she looked at the tree beside her, indicating the arrows with her eyes. I nodded.

"Arrows?" she mouthed.

"Akker's father had arrow holes," I responded.

She shuddered. The feeling was mutual. It couldn't possibly be a coincidence that the man lying in the morgue was riddled with arrow holes and now his son was missing, leaving behind blood and arrows.

"We would do nothing to your children," Qulma said. "How dare you accuse us of something like that?"

"Ask your family. They're the ones causing all this." He turned to the humans gathered behind him. "Now is the time to defend yourself. Don't live in fear or let monsters take control of your life. There may be some people who are willing to lower themselves to associating with these creatures, but I won't. This shit has gone on long enough, and it's time for it to stop. They want a war, and I'm more than happy to give it to them."

That was enough. I would deal with a lot. I had dealt with a lot. I'd had my fair share of idiocy in my days, and I tried to channel that to keep this situation under control and not resort to fighting. But the second I heard Cale start spouting shit about war, I was done. Bad hamburger at a crummy chain restaurant done.

"Every one of you shut the ever-living fuck up and back off!" I shouted. "We tried to get everybody together so we could talk like civilized adults, but if you're going to refuse and keep acting like out-of-control children, so help me, I will put every single one of you in time out. I am not fucking kidding."

"You're going to put me in time out?" Cale asked. If a voice could have the swagger of an entitled drunk man with a sock stuffed in his crotch, his did.

I turned my glare to him. "Try me." He backed down. "That's what I thought. Now, everybody take a breath and listen. No matter what anybody says, no one knows what happened here. All we know is Akker is gone and is likely seriously hurt. I will get to the bottom of it. I will get to the bottom of all of it. But you need to stay cool." I looked at Ally. "You keep things in check."

"Where are you going?" Ally asked.

"To find Akker," I told her.

I looked around for Jonas. This would be a moment when his help could come in handy. He was nowhere. I searched the faces of the crowd of human townsfolk trying to find him, but he wasn't there. Thinking he might have crossed over and joined the Vrya, I turned and looked through those who had gathered behind me. He was nowhere in sight. Weird.

The strange feeling his disappearance created stayed with me as I pushed past everyone gathered in the tight space and followed the grisly trail left by Akker and his attacker.

CHAPTER THIRTY-SIX

I felt the ground move beneath my feet, although it was barely perceptible. It felt less like an earthquake and more like someone moving heavy furniture a floor below. I kept running, following the signs of struggle and small drops of blood. I worried about the blood because while there didn't seem to be a whole lot of it, it was collected together in little groups. Like the victim was being brought somewhere against their will and kept stopping for a moment.

The trail led me around the heavily wooded area leading to the clearing and eventually the Vrya encampment, and out toward the riverbed. Then it went up, climbing the steep hill leading away from the town and heading to the dam. The damn dam. That was where this was going, and where Akker would be. I knew it.

Not bothering to look for the clues anymore, I started booking it straight to the dam. As I crested another large hill, the dam looming beyond, I came upon a flat area overlooking the dam, the city, and the countryside, across from the mountain the mines ran through. In any other circumstance, it would have been a beautiful place where I would have enjoyed laying back and enjoying nature. But there was something horrible there.

Akker sat in the center of the field, battered and bloodied, stripped nearly naked and on his knees. I ran to him, yelling his name, but he didn't respond. It was only when I reached him that I realized he was chained to a large metal stake, holding him to the ground. The chains bound his arms behind him so he couldn't try to pull them apart, and he was stuck facing the earth, only able to hold his head one way or the other. Blood streamed from a wound on his forehead, and he moved so the rivulets flowed away from his eyes.

"Akker, are you okay? What happened?" I nearly shouted, trying to examine him for deeper wounds. His dryad features were extremely clear now, and his body shone in the light. I tried pulling on a chain, but there was nothing to be done. I crawled back to his face and was about to ask him a question when I saw the culprit of the assault over his shoulder.

Jonas stood across the field, a compound bow drawn, and an arrow nocked and pointed right at me. Behind him stood a tripod with a camera facing Akker and me, recording everything.

"Run," Akker croaked, his voice weak and defeated. "Please, run."

"I don't think you should take the advice of a Farsider, Slick. They are known to be untrustworthy," Jonas said, a mad grin on his face.

I was in disbelief, but I tried to process everything all at once. It was one man with a bow. This wasn't complicated math. I was Sara Fucking Slick, and even without the locket, I could take down one dude with a bow.

"Don't move, Slick," he commanded, spitting my name out like a curse. "I know you think you're so smart, so good at fighting that you imagine yourself beating me up and going on about your life right now, don't you?"

"Jonas, this is over. I—"

"Can shut the fuck up is what you can do," he interrupted. "The great Sara Slick could take me down, sure, but the problem is, you traitor, I have this whole place wired to explode, and if you make one move toward me, I swear I will blow it to hell."

I hesitated. He could be bluffing, but the confidence with which he spoke belied a sense of reality, and the risk was too high. I had to try to talk him down. A small, almost imperceptible tremor rolled through the ground. I shifted my feet to get better footing.

"Jonas, this isn't worth it, none of this. We can fix this, we can..."

"We, we, we, we, we," he chirped mockingly, his voice trilling higher with each word. "There is no we. Not anymore. Oh, but there could have been if you weren't a traitor. Sara Slick, the traitor of The Near, that's what they should call you. Of anyone on this planet who should know the Farsiders cannot be trusted, it should be you. The girl who escaped The Deep."

I inhaled sharply. I didn't tell him about that, and I was positive Ally hadn't either. What the hell was going on?

"See, I know more than you think. I'm not some *dumb human* like you think of all of us now. Since now you're so enamored with these Farsiders, Farsiders who tried to frame you for murder, then kill you. Traitor," he spat, his contempt for me filling every word he said, and every time he called me a traitor it seemed to fuel him even more.

He continued, "There are those of us who know the truth. About The Far, about The Near, about you, Sara Slick. I came here to start a war, but when I found out you were here and found out who you were, oh God, I thought I hit the jackpot. Here is the girl who beats up Fae. The one who escaped The Deep! No one does that. If you and I teamed up together, we would be unstoppable. We could rid our existence of the Farsiders for good. The heinous Sara Slick and her sidekick Jonas. I was willing to be that for you. A lesser, a tagalong. If it meant we could start this war and end them, I would have done anything. But, no. Just another traitor of your kind."

Jonas was walking closer now, his eyes wide and crazed. The bow stayed focused on me, and I saw the button attached with a carabiner to his hunting shirt. I was still trying to piece together the camera, and I looked over at it. Jonas noticed and scoffed. Another mild tremor rolled through the ground below us.

"You see, I realized the only value you have any more is your reputation. When you sided with these freaks, it hit me. If I'm going to convince my kind of what type of threat we're under, I had to find them a monster to focus on. A Sara Slick of their own. And I found the *perfect* one."

His eyes traveled down to Akker, and it dawned on me what was about to happen. He didn't choose this place because of the scenery. It wasn't because it was somewhere he loved to be. It was the dam. Akker shook in his chains and tried to lift his head to see Jonas, who stayed behind him like the coward he was.

"I will never be your pawn," Akker choked out. Blood spilled from his mouth as he said it, and he coughed more onto the dirt around him.

"Oh, but I think you will, freak. Do you know why? Because I know what happened to your friends. I know what happened to your father."

I needed to find a way to stop him. He was trying to use Akker's power against him to cause the dam to break, but I couldn't get close enough to him. And if I missed...

"You bastard," Akker said.

"Your father begged for his life, you know." Jonas fiddled with the button in his hand. He seemed to enjoy torturing me by rubbing his entire palm over it and tensing his shoulder, then sliding it away. He was torturing both of us at once, and it delighted him. "Begged. On his knees, not unlike you, right now. Begged me to let him live. He said, 'the Vrya are peaceful.' So peaceful you attacked the people of Hunt when they came to you, right? Hypocrites. He said the Vrya would leave. He promised me, with tears in his eyes, Akker. Tears. But I know the truth. Farsiders lie, and your people would never leave. Not for good. You would go somewhere else and use up resources meant for humans. You would cause us to hurt and to suffer. So, I made him suffer. I cut him apart, Akker. I cut him in every single way you can cut someone. I did it slowly, right here, in this field. His screams went nowhere but into the sound of the water at the dam, and the only person who heard them was me. And I enjoyed every single second, Akker."

The ground was trembling. I knew there was no stopping this. Jonas had won. Akker wouldn't be able to control his emotions, and it would destroy the dam and the town. Then the war would begin. I needed to think fast. Faster.

"Akker," I said, my voice low and even. "Akker, it's me, Sara. You are better than this, Akker. Look at me. You are better than this."

Jonas mocked me from behind and got close to Akker, nearly whispering to him. His thumb settled on the button, daring Akker to move, to cause the righteous war that Jonas desperately wanted.

"And then, he begged me to die. He begged me to end it. But I wasn't done. I hunted him like an animal."

The ground shook and trembled, and I felt it was all lost. I heard the ground crumbling behind us, and the fear of the moment gripped me.

"Akker, please."

"Shut up, Slick," Jonas said. "There's nothing you can say anymore. This is an animal, a creature who doesn't deserve your pity. He is designed to do one thing, and one thing only—to destroy us."

"I know him better than that. He knows better than that. Akker, listen to me," I insisted.

"You sniveling traitor," Jonas spit. "You deserve to die with the rest of them. You're an animal like he is."

Then suddenly, everything was still. Jonas' jaw dropped as he looked around.

"No," Akker nearly whispered. "I am not the animal here. The Vrya are not animals. You are the animal. I will not be your monster."

Jonas screamed in rage and jumped to his feet again. He

pulled the arrow back and nocked it into place. I leapt to my feet and dove toward Akker. I reached for my shield rune and activated it in mid-air, and Jonas fired. The arrow bounced off the shield and tumbled away. He drew another and let it loose, but it also bounced off, and he screamed a guttural curse.

I dove toward him in his distraction and rolled into his legs. He stumbled back, and I stood in one motion, punching him in the jaw with a sweeping uppercut. He stumbled again, and I barreled into his chest, pushing him a few more steps away. His arms hammered on my back as he tried to get me off him, but I threw punches into his gut that seemed to slow him down.

I was overwhelmed with rage and lunged upward with another hard uppercut, and he stepped back in a daze. The cliff was close, and he was tottering on the edge of it. But I didn't want to stop. I threw another punch, smashing his nose and making his knees buckle. He wavered mere steps away from the edge, and I hit him again, sending him back another step.

"This is for the Vrya," I shouted as I hit him with another hook that put him a step away from the edge. His eyes rolled like a slot machine, and he tried to focus. I reared back my arm for another shot when I heard Akker behind me.

"Slick, no!" he shouted.

I paused for a moment and looked back at Akker. His face was a mask of confusion and pain. He wanted Jonas to pay as much as I did, even more, but he also knew this wasn't the way. I turned back to Jonas, who spat blood on the ground and laughed a mirthless laugh.

"You don't have the balls," he muttered through broken teeth. "But I do."

Suddenly, he grabbed my hand and yanked me toward him as he dropped off the edge of the cliff. I stumbled and fell, grasping desperately at the ground to stay alive as his body tumbled over the edge and hung from my arm. I looked down into his face, red with madness and eyes bulging with hatred and purpose.

"Hang on, Jonas. We can get through this. We can fix this together, just hang on!"

"The war begins with one casualty. I will be the face of the resistance. I will be the inspiration for the glorious rebellion. I am The Near!"

He smiled and let go.

As he fell, he laughed and slammed his hand on the button.

I watched him fall for a few seconds. Then an explosion rocked the ground. I stood quickly and ran to Akker while pulling out my switchblade. Explosions filled the air around us, and I knew we were out of time. I cut the chains holding him down, and it broke him free. Gingerly he stood, and I ran, Akker following close behind me. I activated the shield once more, holding it above me as rocks and debris fell toward me.

Suddenly, the explosions stopped. The shield rune was weakening, letting some of the debris through. I looked back at the dam one last time and saw water springing from a hole in the middle.

Soon, it would flood and take Hunt with it.

CHAPTER THIRTY-SEVEN

I wanted to reach out and help Akker as we made our way toward everyone, but he was determined to do it on his own. The fierce, strong young dryad limped along beside me, moving as quickly as he could. Pain etched his face and kept his jaw tightly clenched, but he didn't slow down for an instant.

He knew how important it was for us to get to the others, and he wasn't going to stop no matter how excruciating his injuries were. It was impressive, but also brought tears to my eyes. This was far too much for someone so young to face. He shouldn't have to cope with this amount of loss and pain. He shouldn't have to suffer through this type of fear or feel like the survival of his entire people rested on his shoulders. But he was taking it all with so much dignity.

Wherever he was, I knew his father was proud.

We made it back to the gathering of humans and Vrya and found them right back in the middle of a shouting match. I hoped they would have come to their senses at least enough to not get into a verbal battle while I was gone, but it seemed I was way overestimating their ability to control themselves.

"Oh, you have to be kidding me. You people are absurd." I swirled my hand around, gesturing to encompass all of them. "I mean, there are a few specific ones of you I'm not fully including in that statement, but as an overall evaluation...absurd."

No one seemed to hear me, or if they did, didn't care what I was saying. They didn't even respond to Akker being back. They were too busy snarking at each other and hurling an increasingly stupid string of insults and threats back and forth at each other. We got to the point of one of the humans saying he would turn them into a campfire and toast s'mores over them and I stepped up closer.

"Do we need to go over this again? Shut up! All of you. Time out still stands, and I'm not above hog-tying people to make it happen."

I might have been too hard on them considering everything that was happening around the town and the trauma they'd been through on both sides. But I didn't care. I was sick of the arguing, sick of them pushing back against each other and putting more thought into their hatred for each other than into figuring out what was happening. It was the way fear occurred so often. Rather than pushing through it and stepping up to resolve a situation, people spazzed and lashed out against whatever they wanted to assign blame to. We didn't have time for that shit right then.

They still wouldn't listen, so my only choice was to resort to extremes. I extended my arm in front of me, touched the two moon shapes on my giant-ass metal bracelet, and pulled them together to create an image of a full moon. Twisting it toward me activated the rune and produced the shield. I planned to smash my fist against it to make a loud enough sound to distract the group from their bickering. Instead, when I slammed my fist into it, a blindingly bright white light blasted out of it.

"Damn." I closed my eyes against the glare and turned my head away. "Archie slipped all kinds of goodies into this thing and didn't tell me about them."

At least the blast of light did the trick. Everyone stopped yelling at each other and turned to shout at me, hissing at the light and flailing around. I kept it on them until they went quiet, then smashed my hand against the shield again. I didn't know if that was how to make the light go away, but it was the only thought I had.

Fortunately, it worked. Qulma noticed Akker and her eyes widened, her face brightening before clouding over again when she saw his wounds.

"Akker." She rushed to him. "You're alive."

She threw her arms around him, but he eased her away from him.

"We don't have time. I'll explain everything later, but not now. Everyone, listen to Sara."

They turned their attention to me, and I lifted my voice as loud as I could get it to make sure everyone heard me.

"The dam is failing. We only have a few minutes before we're all under water."

The announcement brought gasps and shouts of fear.

"What?" Qulma stepped back from Akker and looked at me. Her eyes were sharp, staring into mine with desperation like she hoped with everything in her she had misunderstood what I said. "What do you mean, the dam is failing?"

"It's collapsing. Jonas destroyed it."

"No," Shailene cried out.

A few of the other humans shouted, throwing questions at me, but I held up my arm to threaten them with the shield and stop them.

"It was him," I insisted. "He's the killer. He's responsible for all the Vrya murders. He committed the attacks. He knew your hatred for one another would tear this town apart, and now he's using the dam to finish the job."

Cale's face dropped. The fire in his eyes faded and he swallowed hard.

"What do we do?" Qulma asked.

"There's no time to get to high ground," Shailene said, her voice high.

Everyone looked panicked as they exchanged terrified glances and pulled children close. I didn't know what to say to them. My chest ached, emotion tearing at my throat. I was as afraid as they were, and this time, I didn't have answers. Suddenly, Cale stepped forward and looked into my eyes. Where there had been violence and hate, there was now a glimmer of hope.

"I know what to do."

"What?" I asked.

"We run to the mine," he suggested.

"The mine?" I asked.

He nodded. "Yes. There are old access tunnels high up on the mountain. We don't have the time to climb the mountain on the outside to get to higher ground, but if we get inside, the mountain can protect us until we get higher. We need to go in low and block the entrance to keep the water out. Then we hike up to the top of the mountain and use the access tunnels to get out. We'll be above the water level."

"It could work," I said.

"How are we supposed to block the entrance?" Shailene asked.

"We can do it," Akker said. "You only have to show us where."

The other Vrya nodded around him. They were coming together. It might not be in the circumstances I hoped for, but right now, we needed it more than ever before. The dam couldn't hold out for much longer. Soon, all the water it held back would rush down into the valley and swallow the Vrya village and the town of Hunt. We needed to rely on each other if any of us were going to survive.

"Let's move," I said.

CHAPTER THIRTY-EIGHT

The town ran behind us in a solid group. Despite everything that happened before, Cale was now stepping up,
using his voice and his talent for convincing people to get
them to move quickly to the access tunnels. They were low
to the ground, and water had already started to wash over
the area in tiny streams. Those streams would get bigger
soon. Then the dam would burst and turn it into a river.
We needed to move quickly to get everyone in before it
happened.

The tunnel was wide enough for several people to fit
through at a time, and Cale led the smaller and weaker of
the group, humans and dryad alike, deeper into the tunnel
first. The rest of us noticed the sandbags laid out along the
sides and began stacking them in one long low wall across
the opening. A shelf nailed to the wall held lanterns and oil
sitting next to each other. I lit a few to give us enough light
to see and passed some up the tunnel to those who were
waiting farther in.

"Lanterns?" Ally asked mockingly.

"The lights went out with the damage to the dam," Cale said from behind her. "All the electricity in the town is out because of it, I suspect, outside of anyone who has a backup generator."

"Not that it will matter much soon," one of the townspeople muttered.

"Look, our people have been mining here for generations." Cale addressed the huddled group who were working feverishly to lay the bags down fast enough. "If there is one thing we know how to do, it's work a damn mine. Even when the lights go out. Come on, everybody, grab a lantern and get to work!"

Cale made his way back down toward us and immediately jumped in to help lay the bags down, at least twenty feet away from the tunnel's entrance. Ally and a few of the mothers were still on their way back with a couple of the men. They'd left to gather all the children and were still making their way from the town. As soon as I saw them crossing the last section of the access road leading to the tunnel, I ran out, leaving Cale in charge of the group. Akker worked side by side with him as I ran to help get the children inside. Most of the children were across the small stream, which had grown and was now flowing when I heard a loud sound come from the direction of the dam.

"Oh no, the dam. It's breaking right now. Everybody inside," I shouted.

There was a hurried panic to get us all in, but soon all of the children were beyond the sandbags, and Ally brought up the rear with Qulma. We ran into the tunnel together, going past the sandbags and closer to the area where it climbed into the mountain. Once I got inside, I noticed that not only had Cale and Akker created the entire layer of sandbags, but they'd already placed dynamite on the edges of the tunnel.

"We have everyone," Ally confirmed. "We checked everywhere, and we got headcounts. The whole town is in this tunnel."

"We only have a few minutes," Cale said. "Once I light these sticks, though, there's no going back this way. We're essentially causing a minor earthquake. The sticks will go off and weaken this structure here. Then it's up to the Vrya to do the rest. If they can shake the ground enough, we can cause the fault-line to collapse the entrance."

"Where did you find dynamite?" Ally asked.

"This town has been blowing holes in the mountains for decades. There's almost always a box locked somewhere out of the way in every mine in case of a cave-in," he informed her.

"Okay, is everybody ready?" I asked the group behind me. There was a general sound of agreement, and I took it, knowing we had seconds to make this work before the water flooded in and made everything we did for nothing. If we couldn't get this to work, on time, we would have trapped ourselves in our own grave.

Cale nodded, and Akker joined him as they climbed over the sandbags and scrambled toward the dynamite. I heard the sizzling wicks as they lit them, and a few seconds later, they both dove over the sandbags while holding their arms over their heads. Ally, myself, and several of the dryads created a wall of people to block any other impact from getting farther up the tunnel, and I turned our backs to protect ourselves as much as possible.

The Vrya began to hum together, and I felt the earth vibrating beneath my feet. They were concentrating as one, on this specific place, focusing their fear, their pain, their love, all on one spot. It was an intimate experience, and I felt lost in the sound of their hum. I closed my eyes and waited.

A series of deafening explosions rocked the tunnel. The walls seemed to fluctuate, and children cried farther up the shaft. The humming grew louder as the explosions went off, then tapered down and slowly faded away. When the sound stopped and all that was left was dust settling, I chanced a look behind me. Akker and Cale were peering over the sandbags at the entrance. It had completely caved in. Rubble filled everything to within a foot or so from the bags, and Cale and Akker were dirt-covered. Akker turned to look at me, his jaw wide and a smile stretching across his lips.

A cheer rang out among us as the sound of water rushed by the entrance and we saw no leaks, heard no water coming in. I put my hand against the wall and hung my head. I suddenly felt exhausted but elated at the same time. We had saved the entire town of Hunt, but now what? Cale and Akker walked up to meet the rest of us, and Shailene put her arm around my shoulders, giving me the smallest but most gratifying of hugs.

"I know you're tired, honey, but now we have a bit of a hike."

"I'm fine. Hikes are good. I can run a marathon." I grinned. Ally outright laughed, but kept it cool. She probably already knew what was ahead.

"It's about eight miles up, everybody," Shailene said to the group at large.

"Good," Qulma's voice said from right behind her. Qulma's eyes met mine, then moved over to Cale. "That will give us plenty of time to figure out how to live together."

Cale smiled and held out his arm. The Vrya woman took it regally, and they walked to the front of the group. Cale grabbed a lantern on the way.

CHAPTER THIRTY-NINE

The hike was arduous, not only because of the distance but because of the exhaustion which now weighed heavily on me. So much happened in such a short time, and I was exhausted from it. Splinter, who had stayed with Ally when I ran off after Akker, was sleeping soundly in my pocket and I wished more than anything to be able to lay down with him and sleep, too. Well, almost more than anything. A long, hot shower would be number one on the list, followed by sleep. But I would take the nap if offered that first.

At some point, Ally silently helped motivate me to get to the head of the pack, and we now kept pace with several of the town leaders, Vrya elders, and Cale and Qulma, who were in a deep conversation for most of the hike. I tried to listen in on some of the discussions but eventually tuned out as I focused on keeping one foot in front of the other. All around us, humans and Vrya were helping each other over rough terrain. Children, tired of walking, were riding on the backs of the younger boy dryads, two at a time, who smiled and kept their spirits up.

"Should be only a few hundred feet away." Cale broke the hushed tones everyone else was speaking in. A tired but spirited cheer came from the group, now walking no more than four across in the tunnel.

"Slick, smell." Ally had her nose in the air.

I closed my eyes and tried to smell. At some point, one side of my nose had been smashed pretty hard and was incapable of much smelling, but the other was able to pick out notes of clean air and water. We were close now. I only needed to make it a little further.

The remainder of the hike wasn't as bad since the ground mostly leveled out. After one sharp turn where we could only go two at a time, the mouth of the cave opened in front of us. I walked to the edge of it, thankful for the gentle slope rolling down from it in case my weary knees pulled a 'nope' card.

The town lay before us, but it was hardly recognizable. Everything was destroyed, and only the steeple of the small church on Main Street still stood above the water. Some of the people cried softly at the destruction, and Cale sat heavily on the ground. I looked behind to see the rest of the group coming out in the now-rising sun, the soft, blue light of early morning still sharp enough to hurt the eyes for a few seconds after eight miles in the pitch black of the tunnels. Qulma sat beside Cale, between him and me, and I decided to sit beside her, too. She looked out over the town and sighed heavily.

"Our compound will not have fared much if any better.

We were closer to the dam, and the first point where the land is low. I am sure it is destroyed."

"Makes two of us," Cale replied, but there was no bitterness in his voice. Merely recognition, both of his town's troubles and the troubles of Qulma and her people. "What do we do now?"

"Well, in light of the current circumstances," Qulma answered gently, "there is only one option. We rebuild. Together."

"You mean, live in the same place?" Cale asked. I couldn't tell outright if his face told a story of apprehension or disbelief. "Your people are happiest out in nature. Ours like the community of the town. How would that work?" It surprised me. The tone of his voice wasn't accusatory or dismissive, but curious. He was trying to figure it out. For so long I had seen him as a goon, an empty-headed manipulator with hate in his heart, but now he sat here, broken and sad, and all the pretense was gone. All the ego was history. What sat here with Qulma was a man who was changed, forever, and was willing to adapt. I was proud of him.

"More or less," Qulma said. "Perhaps we will be a little closer to the epicenter of town, and perhaps the town could be less..." she searched for the right word.

"Condensed," I finished the sentence for her. Qulma turned to me and smiled while patting my leg.

"Yes, condensed. A little more like our compound, and we will be a little more like the city. Together, we can rebuild and be better than either one of us was before."

"I would like that," Cale told us while staring out over

the water to the town now floating by. "I would like that very much."

A man had tried to start a war here between these people, and very nearly succeeded. Were it not for a brave Farsider overcoming his instincts and the courage of a Nearsider willing to put aside differences for the sake of the greater common good, all the people now sitting here would probably be dead. A war would have begun, and Hunt would have been the first battleground.

Instead, with hard work and the sacrifice of several people, we were now plotting a new town, a new world, where Farsiders and Nearsiders would live side-by-side in peace. It was remarkable. I marveled at the change in the town, and also the difference in myself.

Archie had been right. No matter how much my reputation inspired hate among the Farsiders, they weren't to blame. Not all of them, at least. Hobbes was the villain here, and I'd save all my hate for him.

Ally sat beside me and leaned her head on my shoulder, and I sighed heavily. Soon, the day would begin in earnest, and the Vrya and the people of Hunt would go about the job of rebuilding. Until then, I would sit there with my best friend and watch the sunrise.

And eventually, tacos.

CHAPTER FORTY

Splinter was asleep on the center console again, his body wrapped around a ham biscuit. The horror of everything we experienced was lost on his sweet, spiky little head. At least one of us was at ease and enjoying the drive. I didn't have that luxury. As Ally drove, I sat cross-legged in the passenger seat with Jonas's laptop sitting in my lap.

"Did you find anything yet?" she asked.

I clicked a final button, and his email popped up. I let out a mirthless snort. "I just got into his email. He might have been a deceitful, diabolical son of a bitch, but when it comes to common sense, he was about six neon shades short of a crayon box."

"Was his password 'password?'" she asked.

"Nope. It was 'notpassword.'"

"Holy shit, we almost got obliterated by a second-grader."

My eyes scanned the long list of emails in his inbox. Something stood out to me that made my skin prickle and my blood run cold. "A second grader with a disturbing social life."

"What do you mean?"

"It looks like our friend Jonas had a hot and heavy email relationship going with somebody who calls themself UnhappilyNeverAfter."

"What kind of mall goth, write poetry in blood, listen to Britney Spears when no one's looking shit is that supposed to be?"

I looked at her. "Aww. I miss Amanda."

"No, you don't. She was the bane of your high school career. Well, one of them."

"True." I shrugged and nodded, then looked back at the screen. "I don't know who it is, but they've been carrying on for a while now." I opened a message, and the feeling in my chest worsened. I closed it and opened another. "Oh, wow."

"What?" Ally snapped her head over to look at me. "What is it?"

"Jonas's anonymous pen pal sure had a lot to say. These messages are full of intel on the Vrya. He didn't happen on the community because he was working around Hunt. He didn't discover them and genuinely believe there was a cult lurking in the woods. That's not why he got in touch with you. Whoever this person with the terrible email address is, fed him all the details about them, including where to find them and how to hurt them."

I opened another of the messages and went still. I opened another. And another. I drew in a breath and let it out, fighting to keep my anger down. It took a few seconds, but finally, the rage slipped away. Ally glanced at me.

"Something else?"

"Me. A lot of these emails are about me. They talk about who I am and what I supposedly did. It's the ultimate Heinous Sara Slick propaganda package. Whoever this is, called Jonas up to the front lines against me. And that tells me one thing. I don't know who this person is or how they found Jonas and got him working with them, but Hobbes is behind it."

"You really think so?"

"Don't you think it's convenient to have someone from one of your forums reach out to you to tell you about this strange thing happening? Then that strange thing explodes into a horrible thing, and we find out his email inbox is stuffed full of juicy little tidbits about me? I really can't imagine there's anyone else who would know this much about me, or about what everyone in The Far thinks I did, other than Hobbes."

"When you put it that way, it seems like a fairly astute evaluation."

I looked over at my best friend. She stared through the windshield with a blank expression on her face, seemingly lost in her thoughts.

"Really? That's what you're going with?"

"What do you mean?"

"All this is going on, and you found out the guy you thought we were helping lured us into a trap, and your reaction is 'that seems like a fairly astute evaluation?'"

"Um...that slimy, slithering, son of a cracker salt-licking scumball?"

"That's the spirit."

She sighed. "I'm sorry."

"Why would you say that?"

"I trusted him. This is my fault. I got so excited when he emailed me, and I thought maybe I could contribute. In some way, I could be like you and kick ass and save the world. I felt so smart thinking I was reading between the lines and sifting out these details to figure out he was talking about Farsiders without even realizing it. Only to find out he not only understood it but did it on purpose to lure you to him.

"If I weren't for me, those people wouldn't have died. Qulma would still have her husband. Akker would still have his father. The dam would be standing, and the communities wouldn't have been destroyed. If I had ignored him, none of this would have happened. We almost died."

"But we didn't die," I pointed out.

"But we could have, and it would have been my fault."

"But we didn't die," I repeated.

"Slick, we could have. He manipulated me, and I put both of us and two communities at risk."

"Listen to me, Ally. If this is Hobbes like I think it is, you have absolutely nothing to be ashamed of or to feel guilty about. This dude is a puppet master. Once he decides something needs to go his way, he stops at nothing to make it happen. Unfortunately, that includes coming after me and ending the world—two things you cannot be blamed for, no matter what.

"You are amazing at your job, and you are passionate about it. That's what made you want to believe Jonas. Not some nonsense about living in my shadow. You kick ass in your own right, and I'd like to remind you, you're the only one who didn't completely give up on me after all these years. If anything, the fact that Jonas was able to pull this off and convince you makes it seem even more that it's Hobbes behind all this. It's like him to use his enemies to hurt his damn cause. But you know what? He failed because we succeeded."

Ally smiled. "We did, didn't we?"

"You bet your ass we did. I saw Cale hug one of the Vrya when he didn't think anyone was looking. That in and of itself is a victory. I don't know if the peace will last, but there's a real chance."

Ally let out a sigh and turned a wider smile to me. "I'm proud of you."

"You are?"

She nodded. "You showed that Sara Slick doesn't need to solve every problem with her fists."

I grinned. "You know what? I'm pretty pleased with myself as well. I didn't know I had it in me."

"I did."

Something caught my attention, and I looked in the rearview mirror. Behind us, a car was creeping closer to our back bumper. I knew the face sneering back at me through the windshield.

"Son of a bitch. You have to be kidding me. Pull over."

"What is it?" she asked as the car drifted over to the side of the road and stopped.

"The Fae are back." I unhooked my seatbelt. I got out of the car and started toward the Fae coming toward me. Maybe Ally was right. Perhaps it was my violent attitude that made them hate me so much. Maybe I could put my new diplomatic skills to good use.

"Look," I held my hands up in a show of good faith. "We don't need to do this. We don't need to fight. There has to be some way for us to make peace with one another."

Naida cocked her head to the side and gave me a condescending smile. "Aww, sweet little Sara Slick, the pathetic human. We always knew you were soft. Don't worry. They'll fix that right up for you when you get back to The Deep. I hear the bone pit is looking for some new contributions."

I swung a look over to Ally, my eyebrows raised. She shrugged.

"Okay, these douchebags get the fist."

I grinned and ran toward them.

EPILOGUE

"I can't believe the plan failed," Aldrich whined. "How could that have happened? I thought that human, Jonas, was the perfect pawn. And those fairies you provided with intel proved completely useless. My men found their bodies along the side of the road."

Hobbes looked at Aldrich, an exceedingly loyal Philosopher, but one with the imagination of a thumbtack. His disgust was understandable, if misguided. "He was the perfect pawn. We simply didn't account for our enemy's queen."

"So, what do we do now?"

Hobbes smiled. "I think it's time we took the queen off the board. Sara Slick has outlived her usefulness."

The End

International intrigue. Deadly assassins. Tacos!

Just an average day for the Heinous Sara Slick.
Continue the adventures in *Fight the Peace*!
Coming soon to Amazon and Kindle Unlimited.

AUTHOR NOTES
JUNE 10, 2020

Hey, everyone,

Chris Raymond here.

I am the other half of the writing team of Raymond and Barbant... Or, for this series: ST Branton.

First, let me say thanks. There is nothing we love more as authors than people reading our books. And, if you got to the end of book 2 it means that you like them. (Or you're as stubborn as I am when it comes to finishing.) But I hope you loved them.

We've spent a long time developing Sara Slick as a character, and it's been fun to see her go out into the world and connect with people just like you.

Usually when you write things like authors notes, you want to make them evergreen—able to stand the test of time. This is mostly true for books as well. Don't mention the latest trend, don't lean on some technology that might be here today and gone tomorrow. Remember that author that leveraged MySpace or the used beepers as the centerpiece in his novel? Yeah, generally you don't want to be that guy.

But today, I feel like I have to contextualize these author notes just a bit. Because right now, we're in the middle of a big-ass global pandemic. That's right, COVID-19. Not to mention there are protests in most of the major cities in many small towns throughout the US centered on issues of race and justice.

I'm not raising these issues to talk about them, necessarily. Instead, I want to say this: in the midst of a world that feels like it is completely fallen down, we need little glimmers and glimpses of goodness. For me, I get this from stories. Books. Movies. Plays. Songs.

In almost any form, stories can be a delightful escape from the everyday hurts of the world.

They can be light in the darkness.

I hope that in days like these, you might find a moment's peace. You might get an easy laugh. You might be moved by the hero's journey. You might find rest in these fictional friendships.

Ultimately, this is why we write.

Not always just for escape, but for solace.

When the world is hard, when the hurt is real, we need a balm.

Our hope is that these books could be just that. Whether they're getting you through a world-wide pandemic or just a really crappy day, we hope and pray that Sara and her friends might break the sorrow.

And, if you're reading this and everything is easy breezy... Well may it be the icing on top.

Again, thanks for reading. We love you guys. See you in the next book.

Best regards,

Chris Raymond

PS: Want to hear more from us? Sign up for our newsletter and also receive a FREE copy of *The Devil's Due*, our fast and fun thriller:

https://www.subscribepage.com/chris_and_lee

WANT MORE FROM THESE AUTHORS?

Sign up for Chris and Lee's newsletter for updates, new releases, and promotions. When you join the community, you'll get a FREE copy of their fast, fun thriller, *The Devil's Due:* https://www.subscribepage.com/chris_and_lee

Want more snarky heroines? Well, Chris and Lee also have an urban fantasy series about the mythic gods return to earth in their series with ST Branton, *Forgotten Gods*. The tagline is: *The gods are real, and they're assholes.* And it couldn't be closer to the truth. This series is fun, fast, exciting, and a little irreverent.

Vampires, werewolves, and all manner of monstrous creatures serve the unknown powers of old, but the story centers on the humans who make the heroic choice to fight them. Join Vic and her crew as they attempt to save earth from the gods who want it back. You won't forget, Forgotten Gods.

Oh, and… it is an 8 book omnibus almost always on sale for silly cheap!

While you're at it, we really thing you should try the new and improved *Steel City Heroes*:

A mad scientist fighting the laws of man and nature.

A demon-monster of mythical proportions.

A corporate conspiracy that goes back more than a century.

The Steel City is in desperate need of a hero.

Happy Reading!!